Two For Tea:

An (Off-The-Rails) Ice Era Chronicle
2:30 a.m.

C.M. Moore

www.trollriverpub.com
Two For Tea:
An (Off-The-Rails) Ice Era Chronicle (2:30)
Copyright © 2018 C.M. Moore
ISBN: 978-1-946454-56-0
Cover Design: Virginia Francis
Editors: Ravindra Banthia
Stephanie McKibben

Dear Reader,

Connor and Monica have worked very hard on this particular piece of entertainment. This book was brought to you by hard labor and love. Please respect an artist's work for the enrichment we try to bring you. I humbly ask that you don't outright steal this child born on paper and brought to you by love. If you come by this book by nefarious means and you are simply unable to give the change in your pocket for the purchase price, then take it with my blessing. But if you can purchase it and would like Connor and Monica to continue to bring you great books, please purchase a copy to support them.

Thank you,
Troll River Publications

Other Books by C.M.Moore

Ice Era Chronicles (In Chronological Order)

1:05 a.m. (Ice Era Chronicles) Book 1

Grinding My Gears (An Off-the-Rails) Ice Era Chronicles Book 1:30 a.m.

2:05 a.m. (Ice Era Chronicles) Book 2

Raiden Out The Storm (An Off-the-Rails) Ice Era Chronicles Book 2:15 a.m.

Join the fun with giveaways, updates, and new release opportunities at:
http://eepurl.com/dnoLrr

Dedication

I dedicate this book to my dishwasher, and I don't mean my two daughters. My dishwasher stopped washing dishes months ago. It just sprays warm water on the floor. I have to wash all my dishes by hand, and even then, sometimes, they still aren't clean. Also, now it's making a loud humming noise. The hum makes it hard to write. Here's to being able to afford one that matches my stove…

Acknowledgments

To my better half... Without you, I would never remember the name of this book!

To April, who told me at book club that I could write this novel.

To the Trolls in the Troll River Publishing House. A big thank-you as always. Especially Kris, your support is unbelievably generous.

To Kay, because, you know.

To Amanda, I cannot tell you how much I appreciate the time we talk. It's wonderful to bounce ideas off of you.

To Alison and Diane, you're still here. I'm a little shocked, but it warms my heart.

To my book elf, Shelley, thanks for holding down the fort while I work.

To John Lewis, thanks for acting out the sex scenes in my kitchen. That was weird, but super helpful. You're a good friend.

To Stephanie, for giving me direction and deadlines. Otherwise, I'd just be floating about.

To my daughters, Sam and Capi. You're so supportive. Thanks for sometimes handwashing the dishes.

To Aliah, I hope that one day you're at the helm of your life. You're going to be an amazing woman one day. Always remember that.

And finally, to all the people out in the world reading these stories. Thanks for sticking with me.

To all of you, again, thank you.

Dear Readers,

I'm writing a little note to you about my Off-The-Rails books, but as always, I'm a slow burn. I'll get to that. I promise. Stay with me.

When I first started writing books, it was simply a hobby with my wife Monica. Monica and I would sit across from each other at our favorite café and create. We'd laugh about our characters, we'd play God and toss problems their way, and mostly I loved the way her eyes would shine when a great idea would slip from her lips.

Nothing about that has changed. This is still our hobby, our love affair. I still sit with her and the books can only be created with her at my side. However, as I started to get drawn deeper into this world of ice and snow, I began to learn more about myself. I think that anyone who writes knows that somewhere along the way we can't help but pour out a little of our soul when we tell a story.

And so, the birth of the Off-The-Rails.

Off-The-Rails stories are not only male/female love stories. They can be gay, bisexual, a mix-and-match. In short... different. Things I'm exploring about myself. Things I'm exploring about life. I write these as my own experimental contemplations as well as painting a futuristic landscape that isn't black and white.

Today we live in a world as varied as a rainbow flag, different in ideas, as sexual preference, as in skin color. And since this series of books is set in the future, I can't imagine a world that doesn't still have gay couples, lesbians, or threesomes. To be honest, I don't want a place where these mixes and matches are missing. It would be gray. Diversity adds color.

My Off-The-Rails stories are partly here as companion novels to the times. They add range. I will never tell my fictional characters who to love anymore then I would tell someone on the street who they should be with. These stories may upset your moral compass a bit, but I promise you, I'm writing the correct story for the character at hand. This is their world, their journey, as much as it is mine.

But in case you're not a fan of the Off-The-Rails, don't be worried. 1:05 a.m., 2:05 a.m., 3:05 a.m. etc. will always stay male/female for those who prefer it. I get that sometimes that's just want you want to read. No one will ever have to read the Off-The-Rails to understand the main story line. Without reading the other books you will be able to follow me as we march closer to whether Earth turns into a ball of ice floating in the universe... or warming up the planet somehow and everyone surviving. The books with the time titles will always be the ones where Monica and I move the Ice Era along, but the Off-The-Rails will have their place too. I hope you're cool with that.

Warm regards,

Connor & Monica Moore

~C.M.~

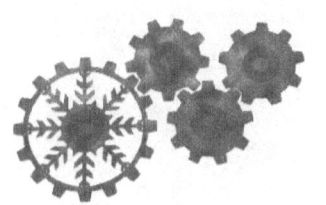

Prologue

Place: Train platform outside Water Base Azul in the Northern Earth Dens, C.T.O.N.A. (Confederate Territories of North America)

Time: 1:55 a.m.

Tea pulled her coat tighter over her blood-soaked clothes. She wove through the busy hallways of her home water base and neared the main entrance. Her eyes stayed glued to the cement floor as she passed the guards. She must get past the men who checked folks into the main gate without being observed. Tea made sure not to make eye contact with anyone. Being noticed was never good. At the age of eighteen, she'd learned that "noticed" equaled beatings.

The bandage around her neck slipped. Tea put pressure on the torn skin near her collar. She prayed the blood flow would slow. Dizziness stole her confidence that she could get out of the base before the H.S.P.C. agents saw the dead bodies. Ducking quickly onto the train platform, she dodged a man carrying a door and noted a set of harvester trains parked ahead of her. She scurried toward the first train right as the vehicle's whistle blew. The ear-piercing shriek bounced off the rock ceiling, but for how loud the sound was, the screech also gave her a surge of hope.

At the last second, Tea changed direction. She picked the train that appeared ready to leave the tracks. The huge vehicle was also a harvester train, but longer than the one she'd spotted up ahead. Her hand slipped over the metal handlebar as she hoisted herself up into the train car. Quickly, she wiped off the blood that streaked her palms using the front of her pants. Once more, Tea yanked her sister's floor-length jacket tightly around her small frame. When she appeared in the first train car, only five men looked up at her hurried entrance. She kept her head down and slipped through to the next area.

The new space had some type of game in progress.

Three men had their pants around their ankles. Their bare asses shone white in the poorly lit train car. Another group of three harvesters was on the opposite side of the area. They threw an oblong orange ball at the genitals of the bent over men. The ball hit the man in the middle. When the ball struck his sack, he dropped to his knees as he screamed in pain. Laughter and cheers went up. Huge handfuls of HOCs were exchanged between the men.

"Who are you?" A young dark-skinned man leaned on a tall carved walking stick. His eyes scanned Tea. She jumped and scrambled out of the car. Tea didn't know what to do, but talking to anyone was bottom on her list. Right now, the urge to fight prickled under her skin, and she didn't even know why. It was time to run.

Ignoring the way her muscles bunched, Tea exited the boisterous train car. When she opened the door to the next room, she realized this space was vastly different than the openness of the previous area.

The narrow hall was strangely quiet, and only one person occupied the tiny corridor. A poised, willowy, woman stood with her back to Tea.

"Mother." From a white pocket door to Tea's right, an older man in his sixties with a stock of white hair came out of the room. The stranger paid no attention to Tea as he scurried down the hall toward the strange lady. The speaker came to a stop in front of the regal woman in the thin green skirt. From Tea's vantage point, the slim woman he referred to as "Mother" couldn't be that joker's mom. This lady was way too young to have a sixty-year-old child.

"Mr. Putnam." The dignified lady inclined her head, but the movement was barely an acknowledgment. "Where is the Snow Flu suit I asked for?"

"My apologies. I couldn't get one."

"That is a lie. Why bother to lie to me? I can see the future."

"No, Mother, I mean it." The older man shook his head. "Honest. I don't have one for you."

"That is more true. You have it, but you're using it and do not want to give it to me." She spoke as if considering every word that left her mouth. "As you wish." She shrugged and then pointed to the door directly next to her. "You can go into my private quarters and give Weaver water as you are. No suit."

"But I… I…" the old man stammered. "I can't do that. Weaver has Snow Flu. I'll get Snow Flu if I go in there. I'll die. Let the harvester die instead."

"You've made your decision."

"Mother, please. What can I do?" Putnam asked.

"Do? You've given the suit to your children. You're using it, but the protective gear wasn't for you. Weaver will have the cure to Snow Flu, and for the greater good, we must keep that harvester alive and with us. Your wife and children must be sacrificed."

"Mother." Putnam looked around the hall like another set of gear would appear. He was screwed. Only the H.S.P.C. had those outfits. "I can get another one."

"You're out of time. Now you must go into my sleeping quarters and care for Weaver until either he is better or until you die of Snow Flu."

"Or?" Putnam ran his hand through his white hair in agitation.

"Or you can die out here." Mother patted the door lovingly. "You will die one way or another for disappointing me. I don't accept anything other than complete servitude. I am Mother, Head of The Originals. Only I know the way the world will heal from Snow Flu. I alone know the way out of the ice. I will stay on this path. We must continue this way if we are to survive the ice that seeps toward Earth's heart."

"I can't go in there," Putnam begged. "I have a family."

Tea found herself holding her breath.

"You made your choice." With a quick yank of her arm, Mother pulled a metal item from the pocket of her long green skirt. There was a flash of a silver blade right before the knife sliced into the belly of the other man.

Putnam stumbled backward holding the knife handle in his stomach. He gurgled a few words and then dropped to his knees.

"Mother," he gasped.

Tea was still staring at the dying man when Mother turned around. Her eyes zeroed in on Tea like Mother knew she was there the whole time. Tea jumped. Her heart started to pound. Even though she wanted to flee, her muscles refused her commands.

Mother slowly approached. The lady drifted down the hall like she had all the time in the world. Tea held the bandage tighter to her neck. Quickly, she tried to read the other woman like she used to decode her grandma when she was in a foul mood. There was something about this stranger, however. Mother was an enigma. The lady could be young or old, tall or short. There was a mystical veil over the stranger. The only feeling she got from the other woman was that there was an essence of power and control that rolled off Mother. If she had only one word to describe Mother, it would be "authority."

"Teagan." Mother stopped in front of Tea. Again, that power wafted from her like perfume.

"I…" Tea stammered. "How do you know my name?"

"I've been waiting for you. You're a little early."

"I am?" Tea glanced around. All she could hear was the gurgle of the dying man on the floor and the swish of the train.

"You've just turned eighteen, right?" She smiled. "So naive for one so old." Mother glanced back at the man on the floor and then to Tea again. "And you're looking for your sister Teresa."

"Yes, my sister." Tea exhaled relief. That's how Mother must know so much about Tea. She'd met Teresa. "Have you seen her?"

"I've seen her. We can talk about Teresa." She pointed to the far door. "But first, we'll clean you up and bandage your neck properly. Once you do a few favors for me, I can take you to Teresa. I help you after you help me. That's how this…" Mother paused. "You like the term *game*. So, that's how this game will be played."

"It will?"

"You'll fight for me, like a junkyard dog." Mother offered Tea her hand. "You'll be my protector. Your gift is growing inside of you even as we speak. Soon you will crave the battles, and I'll give you what you need. You will eat, sleep, and breathe the violence until only two things bring you peace."

"What two things?"

Mother extended her hand a tad closer. "You won't find them on a train." She laughed to herself.

Tea stared at the delicate fingers in front of her. This lady's words didn't make any sense. She also didn't want to take the offer, but Tea had to find her sister. When she found Teresa, Tea would say she was sorry and fix what had happened. "I don't want to fight anyone."

"Soon the urge will take over, and you won't be able to control it." Mother laughed another throaty chuckle like Tea had told a joke.

"I just need to find my sister."

"I've seen your sister. Come with me, and I will help you."

Tea would have to play this game. Her eyes dropped to Mother's outstretched hand.

Chapter 1

Place: H.S.P.C. Headquarters, C.T.O.N.A.

Time: 2:30 a.m. (Two Years Later...)

It wasn't as if Tea didn't know that the head of The Originals was pure evil. Hell, the first time Tea met Mother, the hag had killed someone. But Tea didn't know what else to do. So, she obeyed the old lady and played the game as best she could. She followed Mother... all the way to their execution.

Tea was yanked behind Mother down the long hallway by heavy shackles. Her shoulders dropped, but the weight was no heavier than Mother's invisible bonds. There was no escape.

At the end of the stark corridor sat a metal door with two guards. Behind that door was where she would receive Snow Flu. This was their final destination. Even if she was gifted with strength, she couldn't leave without Mother. She'd had someone telling her what to do since she was a child. Even now with fear in the driver's seat, she simply stuck to her boss. What did normal people do in situations like this? Tea wasn't normal. She was a dumb animal. A junkyard dog.

"Mother?" Tea gave a panic-laced whisper. As she walked, Tea inwardly begged her leader to answer. Mother plodded silently in front of her with a guard at her side. Their feet made a hushed swish against the thick carpet.

A door clicked locked somewhere around her. The clack sounded final. Tea wondered if Weaver was already dead. The other head of The Originals had been taken away at the trial by Snow-Everyone-Joe. Tea gave a sigh of relief when that agent was gone. Even with Tea's strength, Agent Joe had almost killed her. When Weaver and Joe took her down next to the tracks, Tea guessed they were the two things that Mother said would one day destroy her will to fight.

It was a long walk on death row. There was too much silence. Her heart pounded. Blood rushed to her ears. The need to brawl that accompanied her gift climbed. The urge was the only thing that ever ruled her as much as Mother.

"Mother?" Tea raised her voice. "What am I going to do? What should I do?" Tea's whole life was a collage of slavery. From the very start, she'd been drawn into a game she didn't even want to play.

"Stop talking." The huge agent to her right snapped. His hold on Tea's arm tightened as he began to drag her down a hall opposite from Mother. Tea's panic began to rise in earnest. The impulse to hit, to fight these men, doubled.

"Mother!" Tea called out. "What should I do? What about my sister?" Tea planted her feet. The guards around her were forced to stop. Mother would give her a command like she had every day for the last two years. Tea waited. At this point, she was so used to fear, fighting, and instructions that she didn't know what to do without them.

The agent grasping her arm wrenched her wrists. Another agent shoved her shoulders. Tea pulled and then slapped the hand away. The man she hit reeled back. Despite the heavy steel manacles and the guards, she could still move. Tea took another step toward Mother.

"Mother," Tea screamed. Her leader didn't turn her head. "What should I do?"

The head of The Originals strolled toward the door waiting for her. She never looked Tea's way. Mother walked in the direction of the room where she would die like this was all boring. Like it didn't matter.

But their death did matter.

"What about Teresa?" Tea called as the nearest agent jerked her into the open door. All three of the leaders of The Originals were sentenced to receive Snow Flu for study as punishment for their crimes. The word "study" was a farce. This was death. Everyone knew that.

Mother paused in the doorway. Tea exhaled her fear. Finally, the old lady's sharp eyes landed on Tea like she recalled Tea was alive. The cold, sinister glare froze Tea to the spot.

"You're a naïve fool. You always were. Your sister is dead. I killed her the first week I met you. I only ever needed you. You were my junkyard dog, my beast. Now, you're on your own." Without another word, Mother sauntered into the room. The door closed with a final click.

Tea stared after her leader. The pain and the betrayal took up every corner of Tea's brain. Fear ate away at her insides. She was alone. She'd always been alone. Mother had never cared for her. The head of The Originals had lied, used her, and then deserted her. All those times when Tea thought Mother might care for her a little, she'd fooled herself.

The hand on her arm brought her out of her momentary shock. The agent next to her produced a syringe like magic. Tea shoved him. He let go and stumbled backward. She bolted. One of the agents tackled her as she reached the end of the hall. When he caught her, they hit the carpet. They rolled on the floor until Tea's back was pinned flat. The first agent sat on her chest. The guards crowded around her. They stole her air. Breathing became impossible. The needle flashed. Her blood ran cold. Tea wiggled out from under the H.S.P.C. agent and in a panic got to her feet. Hands dug into her skin. When she stumbled backward, the chain on her wrist held her close to her captor. The agent holding her chains strained as she pulled. Three agents hauled her nearer as the fourth pushed the needle into her arm. Blackness edged her vision.

As Tea dropped to the floor, Mother's words on the tracks when they'd gotten captured by the H.S.P.C. replayed in her head. *You're on your own.*

Tea would always be fighting, scared, and trying to play a game where she didn't know the rules. Even now, at her death, she was on her own just like Mother had said.

Chapter 2

Another needle, another pause. Her heart kept beating. *Take that*, God.

Tea tensed her muscles and sucked down her terror. Was that last one Snow Flu? Apparently not. After every needle that entered her body, she asked herself when they would finally carry out her sentence.

If Tea still had her gift of strength, she would have broken the straps that held her arms and legs to the exam table. As she was now, weak as a baby kitten, she could do nothing but watch the needles enter her arm. She'd lost count of how many drugs flowed through her veins.

Time stopped. Fear seized her ability to reason. Fear was the only emotion she knew, and sometimes the sensation was a comfort. At least when she was scared, she felt alive. After being kept so long by the H.S.P.C., she forgot she was human.

The man in the white lab coat whispered over Tea's file to another H.S.P.C. doctor on her left.

"That'll take time. After sixteen hours we can check her temperature."

"Write down that I doubled the dose," the doctor murmured.

Another needle pierced her skin, and Tea wished away the helplessness. Wishing was a waste of energy. She'd not been this vulnerable since she was a child. Now the H.S.P.C. had taken the only thing she had. She was nothing now. Maybe she'd always been nothing. That's what her grandmother used to say.

The doctor loosened the straps on the exam table. Tea was unceremoniously dumped into a wheelchair. Huge metal cuffs snapped onto her bony wrists with a final click. Laughter bubbled up at the idea that these men thought she needed the restraint. As she pulled her arms away, tears welled up when her hands didn't even twitch. When one of the scientists pushed her into the hall, the chain rattled. The jingle echoed and magnified her dread.

Before her captivity, Mother would urge her to fight, to brawl. Now, Tea was alone and empty. Violence no longer was the answer. Hell, she didn't even know what the question was anymore.

Another nameless doctor in a white coat opened the entrance to her cell. Tea offered a muttered curse as he picked up her limp frame. He carried her into her white eight-by-eight jail and set her on the floor. Without looking back, he left her staring at the steel door.

Tea knew this room. She'd been waiting in this H.S.P.C. holding cell for Snow Flu since her trial. Crawling away from the center of the white tiles, Tea considered that she'd once left a woman on the train tracks in almost this same condition, hungry and defenseless. That seemed like a lifetime ago. As much as she could grasp the irony of her situation, the quirk of fate that led her here did nothing to temper her anger.

Tea *was* angry. She let the feeling flow. A part of her hoped the fury would activate her strength. It took focused effort to raise her fist. Her palm made a pathetic thump as the muscles refused her commands. Her hand flopped to the floor. She was furious at life. Tea fumed at the loss of her gift. Last, she was incensed that she had no one to blame but herself. Blame snuggled comfortably with her rash, gullible choices. Not with Mother.

She screamed. The shriek bounced off the walls and landed in the silence. She didn't feel any better, and she didn't feel any stronger. Tea buried her head in her hands and sobbed.

Gathering the last of her energy, she inched along the sterile white floor to the other side of her prison cell. In the corner were lines used to count the days she'd been a prisoner. She didn't have pen, pencil, or any writing instrument. The streaks were etched in her blood.

Huddling into a ball, she dug the chains into her wrist to cut deep into her flesh. Drops of fresh "ink" trickled down her arm. She scooped her fingernail into the crimson stream and created another notch. That made forty-three marks. Damn, over a month now. Maybe they planned to kill her soul first, then her body. Joke's on them. Mother had killed her soul long before now.

After scooting away from the wall, Tea ducked under the observation window on the opposite side of the room. The top of her snarled black hair would probably still be visible, but she would be less conspicuous. It was difficult to be less noticeable with a dark-bronze complexion in an all-white room.

The heavy metal door swung open with a silent swish. Hunger warred with self-preservation. *Not another needle.*

More nameless men brought in a paltry amount of food on a plastic plate. Tea was forced to eat the gray mush.

After, they gave her a host of new injections. While she flailed, the doctors ignored her. They left her in a heap on the tiles. These strangers enjoyed having a live test subject. The constant testing, the drugs, took everything from her. Fear, fury, and guilt were all that was left.

Fight. She lifted her head. *Brawl.* The door opened again. She shifted further back and wearily eyed the entrance.

A beautiful woman floated in. One who hadn't been poking her in the arms. The stranger was tall, regal, with long, fluffy white hair past her waist. Her floor-length skirt swished around her tennis shoes. Dressed in shades of purple, and not wearing a lab coat, set warning bells off in Tea's head.

"Teagan?" The door behind the lady clicked locked.

Tea didn't respond. She always hated her name, and besides, she wanted nothing more than to tap out. Stop playing games.

When Tea remained stubbornly silent, the woman crouched until she was at Tea's eye level. Her palms dropped next to Tea's body as the woman sank fully to her knees. The stranger reached out, and her fingertips brushed Teagan's forearms. Tea jumped at the soft, comforting touch. She shifted away from the petting, but she didn't have anywhere to go. Her head bumped against the wall. The chains on her wrist rattled as if to remind them both she couldn't get away.

"Teagan?" the stranger asked again. "Hi, I'm Luna."

"Hi?" One of Tea's eyebrows quirked. "What do you mean, hi? What do you want?" Tea scrambled to see through the "warm" veneer. She tried to read her new opponent.

"I don't have a lot of time, but I want to talk to you."

Talk? Tea didn't have anything to say. She wanted either death or an escape from this hell, whichever. Her lips pressed into a grim line. After her unfortunate life, was that too much to ask? She didn't have her gift, so she wasn't worth anything anymore. At least that was one positive. No one could use her now.

When Tea didn't speak, Luna stood. The stranger stared out the observation window.

"I'll begin." Luna's eyes flipped to Tea's. "I heard that you were judged by the H.S.P.C. for crimes committed when you were with The Originals."

"I'm *with* no one."

"Teagan, you're gifted with strength, but I'm told that in this prison you've lost your power. You're slowly dying here. It breaks my heart."

What kind of joker was this lady? Tea dropped her eyes to the metal shackles on her wrists. Mother used to say Tea wasn't anything more than a junkyard dog. No one's heart bled for the death of a now-useless animal.

"What do you mean?" Why did this lady come here to torture her? "Did you come here to crush my soul a little more? You're late to the game, lady; Mother did that years ago, what I had left of a soul anyway."

"Your soul is crushed? I see." Luna nodded as if Tea had given her the answer to the most puzzling question of the world. "Nothing left? Oh, Teagan…" the woman whispered as she walked to the door and leaned against the exit. "I think it's wrong to keep you here. Rumi says, 'Out beyond the ideas of rightdoing and wrongdoing there is a field. I'll meet you there.' Do you know what I'm saying now? There are only individuals who make the wrong choices and hurt people."

"Or kill people," Tea muttered when Luna paused.

"Will you be better in your next life? I know you think you're worthless now that your gift is gone, but that's not true. There is so much more than this, Teagan. You think life is all a game, but it's not. We're more than that. You're more than a pawn to be moved around a board. Promise me that in your next life you'll try. I want you to see that there is forgiveness, love, peace. Life is more than fear and anger and fighting. Rumi says, 'When we practice loving-kindness and compassion, we are the first ones to profit.'" Luna dug into the pocket of her purple skirt. When she pulled out her hand, she held a needle. Tea scrambled backward, trying to climb the wall. But there was nowhere to go.

That's why this weirdo was here.

Luna had come to execute Tea. After the months of torture, she would be free of the endless slavery, the terror, and unceasing anger. Tea took a deep breath. Once she was dead, she could see Teresa and tell her sister she was sorry. Maybe then Tea would be able to forgive herself for what she'd done.

This was it then. She stopped clawing at the tiles behind her and gazed into Luna's beautiful face. She hated needles, but at least she wouldn't die alone.

"Yes, whatever, yes." Tea crawled forward. As she grasped the bottom of the purple skirt, her eyes stayed directly on her only way out. Finally, this would be game over. One more needle.

"We're more than the H.S.P.C. We're more than The Originals. Rumi says, 'These pains you feel are messengers. Listen to them.'"

"Yes, sure. Whichever." Tea fisted the purple material until her knuckles paled. Her eyes never left her only real escape.

Chapter 3

Tea thought death would be more… comfortable.

The throbbing ache in her ass brought her to consciousness. Was this Hell? She'd left a woman on the tracks to die. Plus, she'd failed her sister, and her grandma called her the spawn of Satan. She could totally be in Hell. Hell was supposed to be fire and brimstone. Goosebumps rose on her skin. Her guess, not eternal damnation. Her grandma would be disappointed. The old bat was probably waiting for her in the seventh ring.

Tea pried her eyes open. Flickering lights flashed above her. She wasn't dead. *Take that, God.* Her vision blurred, and she blinked over and over. Her eyeballs felt like the inside of a sandbox. Grimy blurred holes came into view. She was in an animal cage with patterned holes the size of a pencil drilled into the top. Light winked through the tiny voids. The cage shuddered. She was moving. Pressing her body close to the side, she peeked out one of the small gaps. *Damn it, if only the holes were a little bigger.* Finally, the world came into view.

A water base hallway zipped past her line of sight. The rumble of wheels on cement clattered against unforgiving stone.

Paintings hung from the walls. Birds, trees, rivers all in warm greens and cool blues. Whatever water base this was, it didn't matter. The only important item here was, could she escape? The idea of bolting flickered in Tea's brain. She leaned away from the side of the crate.

Adorned only in white underwear and a matching stretchy cotton top equivalent of a lightweight bra, how far could she go? She would freeze to death before she reached a door. Escape was a big *if*. Her hands were free, but she still didn't have her strength. No matter. Tea was still a dumb animal. Fitting she was in a cage.

Rubbing the scar on her neck, Tea considered Mother's commands. They never helped. Besides, she was on her own. She would do whatever it took to not return to her captivity within the H.S.P.C. If that meant fighting, fine. If it meant running, fine. Whichever. Just because no one ordered her around didn't mean she was a complete dummy.

Tea scowled at her surroundings. Bring it on. Tea was a survivor. For the first time, she had no one else calling the shots. She could do this. She *had* to do this.

The cart stopped, and the inertia settled. A knock echoed in the quiet hall. Tea held her breath and wished for a way to be free. Wishing never got her anywhere. Praying wasn't worth her time. As a child, she'd learned never to want what she couldn't have.

"Yes?"

"Delivery."

"Is it bedframes?"

The next words were muffled. Tea heard other mumbles and then the cart began to roll. Once more, she pressed her body against the plastic side.

Her eyes focused on the shambles of a water base apartment. The half-destroyed rectangular room was painted in tan and green. Broken and splintered bookshelves overflowed with a mix of books, wires, and tools. Batteries and strange gadgets littered the torn carpet around the fractured shelves. A hole was punched in the wall.

The box jarred, and she rolled on her back. Tea adjusted herself to line up with a new hole. This gap was cleaner than the last spot.

After her eyes went back to the ruined couch in front of the wrecked bookcase, she tipped her head as she swiped at a cobweb tickling her cheek. Near the exit, a man with brown skin much like hers leaned on the cracked door frame. He held a clipboard and a file. His dark eyes appeared uninterested as he ran his fingers through the short black curls sticking up on his head. A blue unlit glass pipe dangled from his lips.

"I need you to sign." The man with the black hair waved the clipboard. The pipe made a clack against his teeth.

"What is it?" a deep voice rumbled.

Tea heard the other voice, but she couldn't see who spoke. Movement caught her eye. Beyond the couch and the bookshelf was a cracked marble counter that opened into an L-shaped kitchen. She angled again. The mystery speaker finally came into view.

The man who came around the counter was a tall blond with massive hulking muscles. His shirt clung to his body like an overzealous girlfriend. When Tea saw him, her heart sank to her stomach. The blond strolled with flowing grace that didn't seem to fit his beefy form. As he came toward the messenger, he tugged on the bottom of his torn gray shirt over his pale-peach skin. His vibrant light blue eyes flipped from her container to the nametag clipped to the courier's shirt. Tea noted the word "Essie" was poorly handwritten.

"Here's the file. There's the package. Sign."

"I want to read that before I make a decision." The huge sexy blond reached for the paperwork. Golden locks fell in his eyes. He pushed the strands back into place with the back of his hand. Even with gifted strength, Tea wasn't sure she could scrap with a guy that big. Weak as she was, her brain didn't offer her a lot of alternatives for a daring escape.

"Name?" The messenger looked down at his clipboard.

"Duke." The blond flipped a red ball in his hand. Tea realized he played with a yo-yo. Harvesters had those. The toy dropped through his fingers and popped back up on its string. The blond tossed the plaything down two more times while he waited.

"I've the name Duke Baron." The messenger handed Duke the file. "Sign here."

"I'm Duke. Baron's my younger brother."

"Younger by one minute. That doesn't count, bro." A second man entered the room. He chewed on a brown hunk of meat as he strolled. Tea had a sense of déjà vu. The man walked with the same casual grace. Every one of his muscles rippled under his crumpled gray shirt. He had the same hair and eyes. Twins. Absolutely identical. Tea blinked a couple of times just to be sure. Yes, even the same sexiness hung around this new addition to the room. Tea might want to run away, but hot was hot.

"It counts," the older twin said. "Probably."

"Says who?" The other twin came to a halt next to his brother and then punched him in the arm. The strike was the type of hit that would've brought down a smaller man. Ouch. These two would crush her. Her heart pounded.

"Says me." They bickered then punched each other again. *Knock it off.* They would have bruises tomorrow.

Side by side, Tea could now see a few differences. Baron's hair was a darker yellow. His locks had deep gold streaks. Duke's eyes danced with more of an ocean blue. Other than these small variances, they appeared to be the same in every way, right down to the fact that they both wore gray shirts and khaki pants.

"I'm Baron." Baron frowned at the man in the doorway. "What's in the old box?"

Tea sized them up. Looking for weaknessess, she considered what she could use as a weapon. Luna's words played in her head: forgiveness, love, peace. What was Tea supposed to do? She was on her own, but damn it, she didn't have a clue.

"Where's Joe?" Duke said more to the name tag. His huge hands flipped through the papers in the file, but he didn't appear to be reading.

"Yeah, where's Joe?" Baron stared at the clipboard over the messenger's shoulder. "Wait, I did order this."

"No me gustan favores," the runner muttered and the pipe in his mouth clacked again. "I don't know where Joe is." He sighed. "Can you sign? I have to go." He handed the clipboard to Baron and then lit his pipe. A curl of smoke floated in the air.

Tea bit her lip and cringed. She prayed that they weren't talking about Snow-Everyone-Joe. What was the chance that they referred to the same agent who captured her?

"We're not signing." Duke glared at Baron and then at Essie. "We like to deal with Joe."

"I'll sign." Baron waved the clipboard back and forth through the growing smoke cloud. "I ordered this." The messenger handed him a ballpoint.

"You ordered a cadaver?" Duke snapped the file shut. He snatched the pen out of his brother's hand. "Why would you—?"

"—order a corpse? Because when I started at the hospital, Doctor Mather suggested it. They got one in Med school on the Uni Base." Baron reached for the pen, but Duke held it away from his brother. "Looking at the cells inside people is different than cells in a petri dish."

Tea's leg cramped up watching them make up their minds.

The word "cadaver" pulled her away from the argument. Was she supposed to be dead? What exactly did Luna give her? Now that Tea tried to recall the pretty weirdo, all she remembered was three words: forgiveness, love, peace.

The messenger rolled his eyes and then grabbed the ballpoint. He held it between the two men.

"Sign." Essie flapped the pen back and forth.

"We don't want a dead person." Duke grasped the writing tool a second time. "What're you going to do with a stiff? You probably can't return it. Remember the bedframes?"

"Bedframes?" The messenger looked from one twin to the other.

"We ordered bedframes from the H.S.P.C. four years ago. They never sent them." Baron grabbed the pen from Duke and clicked it. "Our mattresses have been on the floor for years."

"H.S.P.C. messengers say we're hard to deal with." Duke threw his hand over the clipboard. "We probably need Joe."

"Just because everyone hates to deal with us doesn't mean we can't accept one box," Baron snapped. "Seriously, bro, we'll sign it and be done."

"We probably need to talk to Joe."

"I see." The words dripped past the messenger's pipe.

Tea held in the groan at the mention of Snow-Everyone-Joe. If God ever decided not to be a malicious bastard, today would be great.

"I live here too." Baron's outburst caught Tea's attention. She switched to a new hole with less filth. She lined her eye up to the void.

"You never think things through," Duke shouted. "Zap-my-dangles, dude. Will you think about this from all angles?"

Baron and Duke were in a tug of war over the clipboard. The courier tipped his butt against the door frame. As he smoked, his body language screamed fed up.

Duke nailed Baron in the stomach. Even if Tea had her gift, that punch might have taken her down. Baron flew backward and then jumped to his feet. The envoy hugged the doorframe to get out of the way of the brawl. Baron dropped the pen. He stumbled forward after losing the writing utensil. The clipboard hit the floor next to the beat-up counter. Baron swung at his brother. His fist connected with Duke's jaw. They stepped on the forgotten file. A handful of papers scattered. Both twins dived for the paperwork. Duke reached the pen first. He clutched the writing tool so hard his knuckles turned white. Baron leapt onto Duke's back and wrestled him to the floor. Someone kicked the couch. A new dent appeared in the metal frame. They rolled around until one of them sat on the other.

Tea lost track of who was who. Distracted by the battle, she ran her hand over the scar along her neck. These two could fight, genuinely throw down. *Damn, now what?*

The older one, Duke, came out on top. He sat on Baron's chest. Baron struck him in the nose, but the uppercut didn't seem to faze his twin.

As Duke wiped away blood, he glanced at the box. Tea's and Duke's eyes met. The shock had her shifting away. She closed her eyes. The eye contact was her imagination. He didn't see her. The holes were too small and grubby.

Tea cautiously angled against the side again. Duke didn't seem to have noticed her. Instead, he older brother tipped his head and stared off into space.

"You take forever to make a decision." Baron took advantage of Duke's distraction. "It's an ever-loving box." The younger twin grabbed the document and the pen. "For the love of Pete, bro." With a quick scribble, he signed and then held up the article. The dark-haired runner reached out and took the paper. He tucked the form under his arm with Baron still trapped under Duke's butt.

"Thank you." Essie's words were an exhale of annoyance and smoke. He didn't wait for a response but sailed out of the room. The courier didn't even close the door in his haste to leave.

Duke glared at his brother. His beautiful blue eyes dropped to slits. He punched his twin once more while he got off Baron's chest. Baron stood and then closed the door.

"Are you happy?" Duke walked toward the box. "That guy probably thinks we're nuts like everyone else."

The idea that he might have seen her had her rolling on her back. She went perfectly still.

"I'm ecstatic, thanks for asking." Baron huffed as he faced the carton. "Besides, who cares what he thinks? Everyone hates us. What's one more person?"

"Perhaps I care." Duke held the bridge of his nose. Blood streaked his shirt.

"I don't."

"I should probably punch you again."

"I should pull out your nose hairs with tweezers."

"I'd like to see you try."

Tea held her breath. A hundred questions swirled in her head. If they found her, would she go back to the H.S.P.C.? Fear and indecision held her immobile.

"Where are we going to put this? I probably don't want a dead person on my work table. The stench alone would be like your jockstrap." The older twin rolled the cart toward the door.

"You whine too much." Baron pushed the cart back.

Tea turned her head and found a new hole to look through. Would they open the box now? She didn't want to stay here with a set of combative twins. Her eyes caught the outline of their pecs under their shirts. She could see their nipples poking the fabric. Combative *hot* twins, she corrected.

"This is a mess. You didn't even think about that."

Their voices sounded identical. The only difference was Duke's was huskier.

"I don't know what your problem is. I can still do with some practice. I haven't been a surgical assistant that long." That was Baron. She was positive.

"Four years is long."

"When did you learn how to count?"

They hovered over the box. Tea got an eyeful of crotches. The fabric stretched over what she thought might be a decent-sized package. It had been a long time since she had even thought about sex.

"This says 'open' on this side."

"Look at that! You can read *and* count."

One of them snorted.

Panic set in. Should she pretend to be dead? *Damn*. She couldn't pretend to be a corpse. Could she get away? These men looked huge. If Mother were here, she would command Tea to slaughter them. Look how well that slavery had worked out. Mother could suck an elk's ass.

Tea was on her own.

"You're going to open it?" That sounded like Duke. "Now?" It appeared he wasn't a fan. He would be even less enthusiastic when he realized she was alive. Then again, she thought he had seen her eyes.

"You've a better time to check out the dead body? How about tonight with some candles and a medium?"

"We probably need more people for a séance." Duke chuckled.

Sturdy, thick arms flexed. She didn't have the strength to wrestle with two well-built, muscular men. Right now, a pipsqueak with asthma could take her down. She wouldn't escape. And if she could, where would she go? Maybe it would be best if they discovered her. Being a slave to two men wasn't better than the H.S.P.C. white room. These twins weren't better than The Originals and Mother. Tea was sure of that.

"I got it. You can stand there and look like a pinhead. You excel at that."

If only she had a way to run or fight. Battle or bolt were the only two things she knew how to do.

The lid swung open with a screech before the top banged against the side. The sound made Tea press herself all the way into the corner. She blinked at the sudden onslaught of light. Her eyes fluttered rapidly as a cloud of dust settled. A face came into focus. Bright, twinkling, blue eyes, a lock of blond hair over his forehead, and the most dazzling-white smile she'd ever seen appeared above her.

"Duke's going to kill me." His whispered smirk danced above her face. She tried raising her fist, but her arm simply flopped.

"I haven't yet." A second face came into her view. "Perhaps later." Above her, leaning over the side of the crate popped another handsome male face. "Looks like we don't need that séance."

Chapter 4

"You're not dead." Baron's eyes never left her face. Tea had the urge to preen. When was the last time her thick black curly mass of hair had been tamed? She couldn't remember.

"Outstanding deduction. I can't understand how you're not a doctor already. Your powers of observation impress me." Duke punched Baron, and Baron hit him back. They disappeared out of her line of sight.

Tea took the few seconds to try to come up with an escape plan. Her brain went blank.

Duke's and Baron's heads appeared over the side of the box again. Those smiles warmed her belly. These men were sexier than anyone she'd ever seen before. She hated that.

"Perhaps we should chase down the messenger and get him back here," Duke commented. His voice held hesitation. "You should probably go. You signed."

"We *should*, but I'm not." Baron put his elbows on the side of the box. He dropped his chin into his palm. "Hello, you."

Hello? What did that mean? What new game was this?

"Stop flirting. That's probably not okay." Duke pushed at Baron's arm, shoving his twin's elbow off the container. "We probably can't keep her."

That was flirting? Her eyes jumped between both men. So, this game was where they lulled her into believing they weren't going to hurt her? Nice try.

"Why can't we keep her?" Baron put his hand out toward her. "Hi, what's your name?" His voice had a gentle, coaxing tone. She couldn't help it. A grin pushed at her lips. This situation was utterly bizarre.

Tea glanced down. She forgot. They didn't see a scary, gifted-with-strength fighter. They saw a broken woman in an old, dirty box. Damn.

"Because she isn't a lost item that came in the mail. Stop that." Duke's face vanished again. "We're not keeping a human like a decoration that came from the H.S.P.C. She's a person, not a trinket or a knickknack. We probably should—"

"—explain?" Baron finished. "To who and say what?"

"We probably shouldn't have signed for the box." Duke shoved his hands into his pockets. "We should've said—"

"—what?" Baron glared at his brother. "Come on, bro. Go ahead. What?" He laughed. "Now which one of us is fucking outstanding?"

"You're a dick sometimes."

"Only sometimes?"

Silence.

Tea's back throbbed. She didn't know if she was allowed to get out of the container. Did she have to wait for them to decide? She'd only known them five minutes, but if she waited for them, she guessed she would be in this box for hours. Duke used a lot of *perhaps* and *probably*. That wasn't useful if she needed a definitive answer.

"Can I get out now?" Tea sat up.

As soon as she lifted her frail body onto her elbows, Baron reached for her. She recoiled. His huge hands settled around her shoulders, and he helped her into a sitting position. Long before her captivity, Tea would've hit him for touching her. As she was in her weakened state, she found herself begrudgingly accepting the help. Sitting eased the stiffness in her lower back and relieved the tingling in her legs. Her skin warmed where his hands lingered on her shoulders. She wanted to push his fingers off, but all she ended up doing was petting his soft skin.

Once her head was above the side, she scanned the broken stools along the counter. Duke prowled by the door. She *might* get past such a big man, that is, if she could walk.

Baron held her and shrugged at his brother. He stared for a minute. It looked to her as if Baron's eyes spoke with his twin.

"Are you keeping me or are you going to…?"

Both men stared at her.

"You're certainly not dead." Baron grinned at her.

"We could probably get that guy back here. It'd be the right thing to do."

"*You* could. *I'm* not." Baron turned to her and grasped both shoulders. "Come on, trinket. I'll help you out of the box."

"She's human." Duke bent down to gather the file and the scattered papers off the floor. "I'll go see if I can find the delivery guy. Be nice." With that, Duke disappeared out of the apartment.

"Be nice?" Baron took her hand in his. "Of course, I'm going to be nice to a pretty girl."

Tea's eyes widened. "What does that mean?" No one had ever called her pretty. What was the angle?

"It means that I think you're pretty." Baron studied her.

"What do you want?"

"You could tell me your name."

"I'm not talking to you. Dead people don't have a lot to say." Silence was always better. She wasn't going to speak again. Never show true emotions. Never speak up. Just come up with an escape.

After a few seconds of his hands on her shoulder, Baron spoke again. "Can you climb out?"

Tea shook her head.

"I'll help you." Baron slipped his hands around her back and under her legs. With ease, he lifted her out of the box and into his chest like she weighed nothing. He smelled like heaven. This is what death should be like. Death should be his warm embrace.

His soft words "I'll help you" didn't fool her. She knew when someone offered to help, what they truly wanted. She wasn't a sucker. Never again would she be fooled by pretend kindness.

Baron set her in the middle of the couch. Cushion? She couldn't kill him with that.

After he set her on the sofa, he straightened. Her stomach rumbled. Another one of those attractive smiles lit his face. From his pocket, he produced a chunk of dried meat wrapped in a piece of plastic. He unwrapped what might have been beef and tore off a chunk. Her eyes fixated on the morsel.

"What's your name?" He held out the food, but Tea knew he offered an exchange. The meat for information. Now the game started. Food would be the item he would use to control her. Everyone had a ready scheme.

Tea glared up into his gleaming blue eyes as she rubbed the scar on her neck. He looked honest. She didn't know what to make of the way he stared. She'd never been one to share her past or any of her life. Rubbing the scar on her neck, she would have to find a new way to survive. Fine. She would play along for now.

"My name's Tea." As fast as she could, Tea grasped the meat and shoved the scrap into her mouth. Chewing twice, she swallowed before he could change his mind and take it back.

"Tea. Okay, I need you to eat slower. That's going to make you sick." Baron ripped off another tidbit. She stuffed the piece into her mouth as the door to the apartment swung open.

"I don't know where that guy went. Like a ghost, that messenger vanished."

"Very ninja of him. I'm sure he didn't want to—"

"—talk to us again? That's what I thought; though, it's not like we hit him when we fought. Not like that one time at the hospital."

"His leg healed up fine, bro." Baron handed her another piece of meat. "Don't worry. It's bad for your health."

Duke's eyes jumped to where she sat. "Really, dude? You took her out of the box? Should we do that?"

"Are you kidding?" Baron walked to the side of the couch. Tea turned around to watch the conversation. Even though they were in sync enough to finish each other's sentences, with the way they argued, they needed a referee. "You want me to leave a woman in a box?"

"I thought perhaps you'd wait for me. Because she's—" Duke held up the file.

"—supposed to be dead?" Baron finished. He smiled at her. Her eyes widened. No one had ever smiled at her like that. She couldn't place what was wrong with it. It was so… gentle. Creepy.

"No. Because she murdered someone." Duke's eyes caught hers. "Or people. I don't know how to read H.S.P.C. lingo."

Tea crossed her arms over her chest. If he waited for her to deny the charges, he would be waiting until the ice melted. She wasn't going to say squat. Bring it on.

"She did? But she's squeezable." Baron looked at her, and then his eyes flipped to his brother. His smile vanished. "I want to read that." He grabbed her paperwork and rifled through the documents.

"Killers can't be squeezable?" Duke squinted.

"I'm squeezable?" *Squeezable* wasn't a word anyone had used about her. Ever. "What does that mean?"

"I don't know what killers are supposed to look like. I've never met one." Baron glanced at her. "What do you mean, what does it mean? Is English your second language?"

"I speak English," Tea snapped.

"I'm going to keep you. What do you think, Tea-cup?" Baron grinned at her.

"You can't keep her. She's not a trinket. Even if we want her, we can't own her. You're not thinking this through."

Both men looked at her. Tea shrugged. Her grandmother had owned her. Mother had enslaved her. History repeated itself, and as far as Tea was concerned, they *could* control her. But only until her gift came back. Once her power returned, she would knock the twins out and then leave. If she were lucky, she would find a place to hide. If she weren't, she would be back at the H.S.P.C. HQ.

Tea ran her hand along the scar across her neck. If the H.S.P.C. got her again, she would die. A shudder passed down her spine at the thought of the white jail. Maybe she could navigate the twins until she figured out a getaway.

"You killed someone?" Baron's eyes roamed the file.

"But you're only twenty." Duke shoved his hands in his pockets.

"I'm not saying anything." Tea stared at the cuts on her wrists. So, what if they judged her? Damn them both. Neither one of them could understand what she had been through. No one could.

"Did you?" Duke asked.

The urge to defend herself clawed at her entire being. "I was ordered to leave a woman who had Snow Flu on train tracks. I did it for The Originals."

Tea sank further into the couch waiting for the condemnation and the horror. Never speak up. Never. She knew that.

"Oh, that isn't as bad as I thought." Baron shrugged at his brother, and his nonchalant attitude made her eyes go wide. He slapped the file at Duke's chest. "She didn't like go on a murder spree."

"That's not good." Duke tossed the file to the table.

"A murder spree?"

"No. The fact that she is with The Originals."

"I'm *with* no one," Tea argued.

"You're with us." Duke looked thoughtful. "Why didn't she—"

"—take the sick female to a hospital?" Baron finished. "She couldn't do that. If she'd left the woman somewhere with other people, many people would've gotten Snow Flu." Baron paused. "It would scare the piss out of me if someone waltzed into the hospital with Snow Flu. It'd spread like gasoline poured on a fire."

"You've a protective suit."

"You think I wear a suit all the time?"

"Don't you? You should."

"Don't tell me what to do."

"Timeout." Tea held up her hand. "You jokers are killing me. Am I staying or going?" Listening to the two of them gave her a headache. She wished they would decide. She needed to know one way or the other, so she could come up with a strategy to break out of here.

"We need to think about this. We probably can't keep an H.S.P.C. criminal." Duke shoved his hands deeper into his pockets. "Even if she's cute." He glanced at the exit. "What if one of those thugs comes here to—"

"—get her? I thought of that. We should make sure that no one—"

"—hurts her."

"I don't want to see her hurt. She's fragile." Duke's sparkling blue eyes raked her. "She's so small and—"

"—thin," Baron finished as his eyes followed his brothers.

She wanted to laugh at the term *fragile*. She was anything but. Then again, she would be the first to admit she wasn't in the best form right now.

"She looks like she needs a hug."

"She's only twenty." Duke seemed hung up on her age.

"Did you just say hug?" she asked when the word registered. "What does that mean?"

"We should test your hearing." Baron's brow wrinkled.

"We should probably make sure she's safe, at least until we figure out where to take her." This conversation had taken an odd turn. Duke was simultaneously defending her and trying to get rid of her. Pick one. "And we probably need to make sure we're safe."

"We're safe?" Baron looked as confused as she felt. *For the love of all that is holy, stop with the probably.*

"What if she kills us?" Duke asked.

"Tea?" Baron addressed her. "Are you going to kill us?"

Tea tipped her head as if considering the question. They really thought she would honestly answer that? A short laugh escaped her lips. But her past sobered the fleeting amusement. "Once, I might've done it. If ordered."

"Ordered? By who?" Baron asked.

"I used to follow Mother, leader of The Originals. Her real name was Jordan. If I were still a slave, she'd have made me kill you."

"And now?" Duke studied her.

"I can barely move, let alone fight." The urge to cry dried her throat. Tea wished she had a command. She wished these men would be mean to her. If they would hit her, then she would know how to act.

"Don't cry." Duke moved closer to the couch, and his hand rubbed through her hair. "When you cry, you don't look like a lawbreaker." Duke and Baron even smiled the same. Warm. Beguiling.

"I was waiting for a lethal injection," Tea whispered. If she'd been killed, all this craziness would be over.

Baron came around the couch and stood in front of her. "We'll keep you until—"

"—the H.S.P.C. comes to pick you up." Duke nodded. "That is if they catch the mistake. This'll probably end up like the bedframes. You could be here a long time." He glanced at Baron. "I don't like that the H.S.P.C. would—"

"—kill her?" Baron's eyes captured hers. "I don't either. If the H.S.P.C. shows up, then we can explain that we think she should live."

"Until then, she'll be fine here with us."

"Right, Tea-cup? We'll help you."

"I've nothing to say to two strangers." No one ever offered help without strings attached. She didn't need kindness. She didn't trust charity. Tea didn't know what they wanted, and she didn't plan to be here long enough to find out. She would play along. For now.

"Okay, Tea-cup, you don't have to talk." Baron grinned at her.

"She isn't a trinket." Duke pinned his brother with a glare. "We probably shouldn't call her Tea-cup."

Tea bit her lip to keep from smiling. There was another one of those *probably*'s again.

"Prettiest trinket I ever saw." Baron smiled then scooped her up into his arms. "You're the best thing that has ever come in the mail." He held her close to his body, and she could smell his scent. He smelled like soap and safety. A baffling combination. "Come here, Tea-cup. We're going to help."

Chapter 5

Baron carried her out of the living room and into a bedroom while Duke grumbled over the nickname *Tea-cup*. She ignored both twins as Baron took her into a square room with two mattresses on the floor. Two matching dented bureaus sat on the left. Above one dresser was a display of yo-yos. If they battled like she'd seen in the living room, that explained the broken furniture.

Baron tightened his arms around her and pressed her closer as he strolled past the meager furniture. He took her into a bathroom with a hole kicked in the bottom of the door. Duke trailed along, and when he muttered, she caught the words *probably* and *perhaps* again. He watched her intently with curiosity and concern. After the three of them entered the bathroom, Duke closed the door.

Tea could barely move, let alone kick them out of the bathroom. She rubbed her scar as she considered the open space. She needed a weapon. Fear edged closer to her. A list of horrible ways they could torture her paraded through her mind.

"It's a bathroom, Tea-cup." Baron set her down on a tiled counter next to an oval ceramic sink. "Don't worry. It's bad for your health."

"Still a human being we're talking about here," Duke muttered. "Not a trinket or a teacup."

"You should leave." Tea gulped. "What do you both want?"

"You can't stand up on your own." The younger twin flipped the nozzle on the tub spout. Water began to pour into a huge cast-iron bathtub. Duke shook his head then turned around and opened the toilet. He pulled his cock out and began to piss.

Shocked, Tea turned her face as her cheeks began to heat. Intently, she studied the counter where she sat. She wasn't a virgin, but even Harvesters had the common decency to do that alone. Her eyes popped to Baron.

Baron paid his brother zero attention. He stared at her wrists. Baron wasn't just staring, that wasn't the right description. Baron's eyes had an intense gaze as he examined the cuts. He glanced up briefly and caught her watching him.

"I'm gifted with seeing on a microscopic level. I'm studying the cells and looking for infection," Baron murmured more to her palms then to her. He glanced up at her face. He tipped her chin back and forth as his eyes dipped to her neck. She knew she had a scar there, but he was scrutinizing the mended flesh intently.

"Who slit your throat?" Baron asked suddenly.

Tea threw herself off the counter by reflex, but weakness held her legs hostage. She wasn't strong enough to hold herself up. She ended up almost collapsing on the floor.

Almost.

Baron's hands snaked out and caught her around the waist. The feeling of his warm embrace was so alien to her she didn't know what to do. She went perfectly still.

"It's okay, Tea-cup." Baron held her close and stroked her hair.

"I'm not talking to you." Tears gathered, and she sucked them down. These men made her entire body tense.

"Fine," Baron agreed.

"Don't talk," Duke added.

"What do you want from me?" she whispered.

"Shush, Tea. Nothing." Baron smoothed her hair back. "I'm not going to hurt you."

"I'm not that easy to trap. I know how the world works." Just wait, he would hurt her sooner or later like everyone else.

"We're not trapping you."

"This is what I'm talking about, Baron," Duke muttered and tucked his dick back into his pants. "You never think things through, dude. You can't go around saying whatever is in that dumb head of yours." Duke flushed and turned to face his brother. "Someone slit her throat?"

"Never mind. It bothers Tea, and close the toilet seat, bro." He motioned to his brother. "Don't leave the lid up, we have—"

"—a woman around now." Duke snapped the lid down. "Got it."

Baron gently took her into his arms again and picked up her legs. He carried her to the now-filled tub and sat on the edge. Duke turned off the tap and then leaned against the wall with his hands shoved into his pants pockets. Steam misted above the waiting water.

"We're going to take off these clothes." Baron's voice was somber and stern.

That sounded about right. Everyone fucked you over at some point, either figuratively or literally. This gentleness was all an act.

"No." Tea gave an adamant refusal. Her clothes would stay right where they are. The light fabric wasn't much, but this was better than naked.

"No." Duke's refusal came at the same time as hers. Baron's head whipped around to look at his twin.

"What do you mean?" She stared at Duke as well.

"What do you mean, what do I mean? I mean no." Duke frowned. "I said it clearly."

"Why? Didn't you see the box? She's a mess." Baron held up a dirty piece of her hair. "These clothes are rags. What about infection?"

"It's probably wrong—" Duke shoved his hands further into his pockets.

"—to undress her?" Baron finished the sentence. "I know, but I work with patients every day and some things are necessary. When have you ever been—"

"—shy?" Duke muttered. "I'm not shy. It's not me I'm thinking about. We should probably consider what we are doing before we do it."

"It's not sex, it's—" Baron sat on the side of the tub and adjusted her in his arms.

"—her care. I get it, but I'm not sure."

"You're never sure about anything. For the love of Pete, I'm not going to wait a hundred years while you say *probably* and *perhaps* and never figure anything out. She needs to be clean, and she can't take a bath by herself right now."

The finishing of the sentences was starting to seem natural to her, but her present fear of being at the mercy of these two huge men held all her attention. She shook her head. Who was she kidding? She was their captive, clothing or no clothing, and there was nothing she could do about it. Her life was no better than when she was a prisoner of the H.S.P.C.

God was a mean-spirited bastard.

"I wish I could kill you," she whispered through her clenched teeth. "Bring it on." Tea could make it through this next horrible ordeal.

"We're trying to help you." Baron's hands slid around to the front of her body. She tensed until her muscles hurt. Tears rolled down her cheeks, and she worked to conjure her fighting attitude. What they were doing reinforced her being right. Everyone on this planet was sadistic.

"What do you want from me?" She squirmed until her muscles ached. Her arms dropped to Baron's chest. "What is this?"

"We don't want anything, Tea." Duke tipped his head to the side. "This is—"

"—a bath." Baron's fingers slipped under the fabric of the stretchy tank top. He pushed the top up and over her head.

Tea gulped back the dread and the humiliation. Oddly, when they took off all her clothes at H.S.P.C., it didn't feel as intimate as this. Stripping her now felt like they exposed all of her. Not only her body, but her soul. Baron's hands went to her underwear next. She considered struggling, but that wouldn't make any difference.

"Please." Tea hated to beg. The whispered plea was barely audible. She tried to spit on him, but her mouth was too dry. "Do you enjoy this? Hurting me?"

"He's not hurting you." Duke leaned away from the tub and pulled out his yo-yo.

"You have cuts that are dirty." Baron slipped off her underwear. "You've got caked blood on your skin. These clothes need washing. I promise you this is only a bath."

Baron held out her top and underwear to his twin. The cloth was no longer white. The underarms were soiled. Gray splotches mixed with brown stains. They would be lucky to get it clean again. Baron's clothes brushed her skin. She closed her eyes and waited for the assault. When she killed them, she would make their death long and painful to make up for this.

"She doesn't believe me because you look like a gorilla." Baron glared at Duke. Tea's eyes fluttered open.

"I'm a gorilla?" Duke took her two garments and then opened a closet next to the toilet. Inside, she noted a washer and a dryer stacked on top of each other. He threw her clothes in the washer and punched a button before he slammed the door.

"It's that dumb face of yours." Baron stood with her still clutched in his arms.

"You do know that you look identical, right?" For a moment being naked didn't seem as important as pointing that out.

"You're the ugly one." Duke dropped his yo-yo down and then bounced it back up.

"You look the same," Tea repeated.

"He's a gorilla. All cagy and hairy. You're looming." Baron huffed at his brother. "Why can't you be comforting for Tea?"

"I could be comforting if I wanted." Duke slipped the toy back into his pocket.

"Come on, bro. Do that. Say something soothing."

"If I wanted to say something soothing, I'd do it for her, not for you."

"Then say it for her," Baron growled.

"Timeout." Tea tried to hold up her hand, but it fell into her lap. Both men looked at her. She shook her head. "I'm not talking to either of you."

"As much as I'd prefer to keep bugging you." Duke glared at Baron. "I probably can say something comforting." Duke paused as if considered every word in the English language. "Tea, I'm not going to hurt you. Neither is that bag of bolts holding you. Baron's a pinhead." He smiled. When she didn't smile back, he studied her face. "I promise, I'm not going to hurt you." Duke shoved his hands into his pockets. "Don't cry, okay? When you get all weepy, you don't look like a felon."

"Ha." Baron grinned. "That was the worst soothing I've ever heard." He gathered her closer to him. She held onto his neck.

"I'm not so good at talking to women," Duke muttered.

"You're not good at talking," Baron snapped.

"And you are?"

"Better than you."

"Timeout." Tea agreed with Baron that Duke's speech wasn't comforting, but she thought Baron should stop picking on his brother. He tried.

"As long as you feel better, Tea-cup. You can relax. We're helping."

"She's a cute felon," Duke added.

These two were a bizarre pair. Every time she prepared herself for how terrible they would be, they surprised her. Cute and felon didn't belong in the same sentence.

"I'm sorry this is difficult, but the bath needs to be done. That box was filthy, and you're too weak to do this by yourself." Baron's eyes met Tea's. All she could find in that look was concern. What was the gimmick? "I'm a surgical assistant, and I work at the hospital. Infection is a real problem living underground. I'm here to help you." He held her out above the edge of the cast iron and then sunk her ankles into the tub. The water was scalding. They planned to cook her alive. Figures.

"You say help. You mean boil." Tea climbed back into his arms, but he still lowered her until her calves sank. The water was too hot. Her skin tingled with pain and heat. "You're burning me."

"Ha." Baron chuckled. "It's not that hot, Tea-cup."

"For an outlaw, you're a wimp." Duke gave her a pointed look. *Damn.* She gritted her teeth and didn't say anything as Baron slipped her the rest of the way into water that was boiling off her skin. She glared at Duke.

"See?" Baron smiled at her like he was oh-so-proud of her. "We're helping." He kissed the tip of her nose before he dumped soap into the water.

Once she was in the tub, he headed to the closet and rummaged around. His back turned as if he trusted her. She wanted to laugh. As soon as she had her gift back, these two would be obliterated.

The washer banged out a hypnotic beat. Duke sat on the counter and played with his yo-yo. His eyes scanned her. If he wanted her to talk, she wouldn't. They were enemies. Probably. *Damn, now he had her doing it.*

Her muscles relaxed as she sank deeper into the tub. Her eyelids drifted closed of their own volition. A sigh escaped. Tea worked to gather her fear to keep her ready for the horrific violence ahead of her. The water lapped at her skin. Fine. She would admit it to herself. The water wasn't *that* hot. The warmth soothed all her aches.

"Lean over." Duke's deep rumble pulled her out of her calm. Her eyes popped open. He'd taken off his shoes and socks and rolled up his pants. He held a plastic bottle. "I don't think Baron has thought this through, but you're in the water now."

"What do you mean?" Her eyes flipped to the soap.

"I mean lean over." Duke didn't wait for her to move but stepped into the tub. "You probably do need a hearing test."

"My hearing is fine." Tea scooted all the way over to accommodate his ski-sized feet. While she was plastered to the side trying to dodge him, he sat down on the edge of the tub. Duke grasped her shoulders as gently as Baron.

Duke arranged her between his legs and placed both feet next to her ass. She tried desperately not to think about what he could see and what the top of his feet brushed.

"Your hair looks like you got shocked by one of Duke's batteries." Baron walked back into the bathroom holding an enormous white robe in his hand. "I don't have any clothes for a woman."

"Perhaps that's the real reason the H.S.P.C. sent her here. They gave up trying to tame her hair." Duke laughed at his own joke. "My robe is fine. If Tea wants it, she can have it. She can have whatever she wants."

Tea watched his hands travel up, up, and up until he started rubbing her scalp. Duke's fingers massaged the top of her head, then her temples and down to her shoulders. His hands were rough, callused, and amazing. Strong yet tender. Her standoffish resolve softened. Where was Tea's kill or be killed instinct? It might have floated away in the warm bath. Her eyes closed as he stroked her. She exhaled. This was nice. They appeared to be nice. *Damn.* She didn't know what to do with that.

Tea's hands slipped up Duke's leg, and she leaned into his thigh. Sleep invited her to keep her eyes shut. He kneaded the stress and fear out of her. Duke caressed her shoulders. Warm water sloshed over her hair.

"Ahhh." She tried to hold in the moan, but the groan found freedom. Baron chucked and then walked back out of the bathroom.

"Don't tell Baron, but I thought I saw you in the box, Tea," Duke murmured in her ear as soon as his brother left. His fingers patted her hair. "I didn't think it was right to lie to the delivery guy, and I'm still not sure if any of this is going to work, but there's something about you. You're kind of sweet for an H.S.P.C. lawbreaker. I want to keep you. Probably shouldn't want that."

Sweet. Another word no one had ever called her. Sooner or later, these men would find out who she was. They would discover she would never again be a slave, but for right now, Duke's massage was simply too relaxing to think.

Chapter 6

Tea woke in a bed. She hadn't been in a bed for longer than she could remember. Hell, she hadn't been in the same place for longer than one or two nights since she was a kid.

As she rolled over, her robe tangled with the blanket pulled up to her chin. The way the fabric pulled around her neck felt like someone was strangling her. Tugging, she shoved the cloth down. Glancing around the bedroom, she recalled the blond twins. She was in one of their beds on the floor of their room. The other mattress was empty.

Tea was about to jump up and run, but stopped. Pausing, she clenched her hands into fists. She didn't have her gift of strength. She wouldn't be able to battle the twins in her reduced state.

As she pushed hair away from her face, neatly wrapped bandages around her wrists caught her eye. For now, she would sit here, and she hoped if she rested enough, her gift would return. She would stay in bed.

Her bladder begged to differ. Tea stood. Stumbling, she shuffled to the bathroom. After relieving herself, she stood in front of the mirror above the sink. Her skin was pale, and her hair was a black fuzzy nest on top her head.

Duke said she was "sweet." She didn't look sweet. She looked haggard. Her fingers brushed through her snarled mess. On a whim, she looked for a brush. Tea opened the drawers one by one. She found scissors. Gripping the metal handle, she hacked at the parts of her hair that could never be tamed.

When her curls fell to her shoulders in softer waves, she set the scissors on the counter. The shears laughed at her. She could use them as a weapon. When she picked them back up, the metal felt cool in her palm. If she stayed, these men would hurt her. Killing them is what Mother would tell her to do, but look how her vicious commands had turned out. Luna's words replayed in her head: forgiveness, love, peace. Tea didn't know how to do those things.

The door to the bathroom opened behind her. She jerked and spun clutching the metal shears.

Duke entered first. Due to two years of ingrained habit, she dove for him. She had the metal to his neck before he even spoke a word.

"You're awake," Baron said from behind his brother. She detected a faint snicker.

"Another one of Baron's brilliant deductions." Duke stayed motionless but his eyes caught hers. They glowed bluer this morning with edges of teal. Magnificent. Her breath hitched.

"Better mobility." Baron grinned. "You should do some stretches. Duke and I do yoga daily. It's supposed to help with our anger issues."

"We tend to fight." Duke's eyes danced. "I don't know if you've noticed." If he was concerned about her threat or the shears at his throat, he didn't look it. He looked *delighted*.

"I don't care what you do or don't do. Fuck yoga. I'm leaving." Years of living on the run felt natural. This relationship, whatever it was, didn't feel right at all. Her hand trembled, and so did her bottom lip. She tried to flex her fingers, but she couldn't.

Duke's broad chest was too tempting. She bit her bottom lip to stop from shaking. She refused to cry. These men were nice to her. Compassion was as foreign to her as the bed she'd slept in last night.

As soon as her eyes dropped to Duke's chest, Baron entered the bathroom. She glanced at the younger twin. Duke stepped to the side and brought his hand up, sweeping his arm and knocking the scissors to the floor. Duke grabbed her wrists once there was nothing at his jugular. These men were true fighters. With little effort, he flipped her around as he pinned both her hands behind her back.

Now Tea faced Baron. Duke pressed her back to his hard chest. She couldn't move. Baron hopped up next to the sink.

"Leave me alone." Tears gathered. "I'm not talking to you." She wasn't strong enough to fight them. She hadn't been this weak since she was a child.

"I wish we could leave you alone, Tea." Duke exhaled. "But you're with us now, and—"

"—you need help whether you admit that or not," Baron finished.

"I'm *with* no one." Tea struggled against the hold.

"She tried to cut my throat *and* leave. That's a good sign. You're getting your energy back," Duke's voice rumbled. "But still as weak as a dying battery, kind of like you." Duke glanced at her and then smirked at his brother.

"If you want to check out something stupid, there's a mirror above the sink." Baron pointed behind him.

Again, Tea wanted to point out that they were identical.

"Let me go," she snapped instead.

"Don't mess up the bandages on her wrists. I wrapped those twice." Baron slipped off the counter and stepped toward her. "Duke will let you go after I'm done with you."

"Bring it on, you bastards. You jokers will see." Tea prepared herself for the hit. She squeezed her eyes shut. She felt Baron move closer. Now he would hit her to remind her who was in charge. At least if one of them punched her, the world would be normal again.

When nothing happened, she popped one eye open. This was exactly like last night when they didn't take advantage of her weakened state. She squinted. What in damnation was the matter with them?

Baron stared at her with his head cocked to the side. Again, he looked as though he peered inside of her. A shiver raced down her spine. Baron dug into his pocket and pulled out a plastic tube. She moved her head, but he reached out and lightly dragged the tip of the device across her forehead.

As he looked down at the screen on the side of the gadget, she chanced a quick glance up at Duke. He grinned down at her.

"I like your hair. Perhaps we can find a brush. I probably got one." Duke didn't let go of her hands, but his firm hold didn't hurt. He didn't sound furious that she'd tried to kill him. She was a murderer, and they treated her like a, well… a teacup.

"All you have to say is you like my hair?"

"It looks better. And those scissors are probably not sharp. I'm surprised they cut those dreads."

"Probably?" Tea shook her head slowly. Hanging with these two men was like spending time with lunatics. "What do you mean?"

"What do you mean, what do I mean?" Duke wrapped an arm around her waist. "Am I not enunciating?"

"I'm not talking to you." Tea exhaled.

"I think it's cute you say that."

"Her temperature is still dropping. I don't know why." Baron held up the object in his hand.

Funny, she didn't feel cold.

"You work in a hospital. Venture a guess." Duke hugged her to his rock-hard frame. She could smell metal and man. Her whole body began to relax even though she fought the growing calm. He was so warm that she pressed her ass into him.

"I'm only in surgery because of my gift. I don't know enough about all these medications. I have the books to study, but I don't know. Did you see the file? It's like reading the who's who of mystery drugs. It was easier when I worked categorizing organisms."

"We probably should—" Duke began.

"—put her back to bed," Baron finished.

"Come on, little Tea." She was scooped up in Duke's arms like she was a bag of potatoes. She had that same feeling of safety as when Baron carried her. Duke hauled her back to the bed. He set her down and then pulled the covers up to her chin. She wasn't cold. A second shiver shot down her spine. Okay, maybe she was a little cold.

"What's wrong with me?"

"Nothing." Baron grinned.

"You're cute and spunky. Like eighty amps straight to my system." Duke dug through his closet.

Tea's eyes widened at the compliment. What the hell did "eighty amps" mean? Fuck it. She wasn't asking.

"Don't worry. It's bad for your health." Baron walked out the door. She wished she had the scissor to throw at them.

Just as Tea decided to make them explain what was going on, Duke bent over. His ass was made for exploring. Tea licked her lips while she pictured Baron bent over next to his brother. She smiled thinking of them side by side. Her twins could make a Tea sandwich.

Tea's smile switched to a scowl. Had she just thought *her* twins?

"I called the hospital on the water base connection line." Baron came back into the room. "I talked to Doctor Mather." He held the document that the courier brought.

"You called your boss?" Duke straightened and spun around. "Why?"

"We need medical advice, and he's a doctor as well as a surgeon. I don't know about these drugs. I can see the change in her, but I don't know what it signifies or what we should do about it."

"Did you tell him she was here?" Duke's voice sounded like it held genuine fear. Tea had no idea what kind of bad things would happen if the H.S.P.C. found out they had kept her when she wasn't dead.

"Of course, I didn't say Tea was here."

"What did you say?"

"I told Mather that you went off the deep end and tried to commit suicide. I told him you took all these pills. Then I rattled them off."

"You did what?" Duke exploded, but Baron didn't look up from the file. He paged through it. "This is what I'm saying. Zap-my-dangles, Baron, will you please think before you speak?"

Tea laughed and then sobered.

"Doctor Mather said he figured that you'd cracked. He said you were clearly unhappy here. Is that true?" Now Baron looked up from the file. Both brothers appeared angry. Duke's skin flushed with ire. If she were Baron, now would be the time to run for cover. Then again, Baron looked like he might punch his brother with only a slight provocation. She leaned back on her pillow and decided their battles weren't her problem.

"If I'm unhappy here, it's probably beside the point. You told Mather I went off the deep end. Outstanding lie you thought of. Good to know you made me the insane one."

"You wanted me to be the insane one?"

"You already are."

Tea held up her hand. "Timeout. Can we talk about me?"

"Mather said that this drug..." Baron rifled through some pages. "Calizopenipine. That's the one that makes your temperature drop. He said it's in its test phase right now. The side effect of the drug is your body replicates hypothermia. He asked me how you got an antipsychotic drug to begin with."

"What?" Duke stared at her. "The H.S.P.C. thought our little Tea was psychotic?" Duke's brow wrinkled. "But she's so delicate."

"First off, I'm not 'your little Tea.' And second, it wasn't like I asked for the drugs. They kept me as a live test subject after my trial. I was a human pincushion." As she hugged the blanket to her shoulders, she shuddered at the recollection. She wasn't sure if she was cold or the memory was horrific. Most likely both.

"I didn't know they did that." Duke pulled up her blanket. "That was probably wrong, Tea."

"Not probably. It was wrong." Baron sighed and held up the file. "According to this, they also gave Tea allergy pills for cat dander, but I doubt Tea was—"

"—spending time with felines?" Duke asked. "Right. So, what else did Doctor Mather say?"

"He went on and on about serotonin and thermoregulation. I followed along in my book as much as I could." Baron stopped suddenly and looked at her. "Tea? Do you have any brain damage?"

"I think listening to the two of you might give me brain damage."

Duke chuckled. "For a woman who doesn't smile much, it's a shame. You're beautiful like that."

"I'm not talking to the two of you." Tea rolled eyes.

"Ha." Baron grinned with a warmth that chased the chill away from her bones. "I think it's funny when you say you're not talking to us."

His smile made her squirm. She wasn't sure if she liked it or not. The look was downright unnatural. The flattery from Duke was strange too.

"What do we do?" Duke asked his brother. "What did Mather suggest?"

"Mather said to treat for mild hypothermia and keep checking your temperature." Baron held up his hand. "I mean her temp. Not yours. If it gets too low, we should bring you to the hospital. I mean her, not you."

"Where's the electric blanket?" Duke asked.

"I gave it to Sigrid for his iguana."

Silence. The two men stared at each other in another one of those private wordless conversations.

Tea didn't like that. It was better when the two men talked out loud. The silence felt surreal. Actually, this all felt surreal.

"So, what does this mean?" she asked when neither man spoke again. "I have hypothermia?" She didn't feel cold. She felt fine. Another shiver surged to her toes. Not fine, but she was in a bedroom, not on the surface of the planet. She couldn't have hypothermia.

"It means that an iguana is using our electric blanket," Baron tossed out.

"And you made me look like a mental patient with your fancy doctor friend. That's a low blow, dude." Duke crossed his arms over his chest. "I'm going to punch you for that."

"Fine. Do it. Go ahead." Baron egged on his brother. "Come on, bro."

Duke grabbed Baron by the front of his shirt. Baron shoved his brother's hand away.

"Timeout." Tea couldn't help the bubbling mirth. She snorted. She could be dying for all she knew, but to get a straight answer out of these two would take a lifetime. Duke would add *perhaps* and *probably* to his sentences until she wanted to slap him.

"Tea, don't wor—"

"If you tell me not to worry one more time, it's going to be bad for *your* health." She huffed. "Now are you turning me into the hospital?"

"If you get colder, we'll have to take you to the hospital." Baron didn't look happy about that idea. "We'd have to, Tea."

She wasn't happy about that either.

"If we take her to the hospital, they'll probably take her back. I want to keep her." Duke stepped in front of the door like he would stop Baron if he tried to remove her.

Tea held in her grin. As long as she was here with the boys, she could plan an escape. She didn't want the H.S.P.C. to capture her again. That was one game she didn't want to play again. Whatever she had to do to make sure that didn't happen, she would do it. That included playing nice with these jokers.

"I'm glad you like her." Baron walked over to the closet near the dresser and scanned the contents.

"Right now, I like her better than I like you." Duke grabbed a yo-yo and flipped it through his fingers. The action was like an uncomfortable fidget. He made a triangle with his fingers and spun the toy.

"If she gets too cold, they can take all the blood out of her body, warm it, and then put it back in." Baron's voice was muffled from the closet, but Tea heard the explanation. She recoiled at the thought.

"What? No." Duke's face screwed up into a grimace. He slapped the yo-yo down on the dresser.

"I'm not going near another needle. Go lick a caribou." Under the blanket, Tea wrapped her arms around her body. "I'd rather be cold and die. Leave me alone."

"You don't mean that, Tea-cup. You don't want us to leave you alone." Baron raised one eyebrow like he dared her to deny it.

"We're here to help you. We're not going to let you die." Duke appeared troubled by the thought. She wanted to make fun of him for putting his emotions out there for her to see. That was a dangerous action if ever there was one.

"If you're going to stay here and let us hide you from the H.S.P.C., then you're going to have to accept us warming you." Baron stared into her eyes when she remained silent. "Say the word. Stay and let us protect you. No attacking us with scissors. It's either that or you go to the hospital. What do you want?"

Say the word? She considered his offer. Baron's hard stare was clear. She recognized a shakedown. The younger twin just told her she would have to do what he asked if she wanted to stay away from the hospital and be subsequently sent back to the H.S.P.C. Giving in to someone in exchange for something wasn't a new concept to her.

Fine. She would play the game.

"Are you going to let us help you?" Duke asked. "Say the word, Tea." Duke's eyes flipped to Baron and then back to her. "Say you'll be with us."

"Yes. I'm with you." Tea exhaled. *Damn.* She would have to see how this game would work out. "My blood stays in my body where it belongs. I'll stay here, but I'm not talking to either of you."

"Fine." Duke grinned at her.

"Then," Baron nodded, "we will keep you warm until you feel better."

Chapter 7

Tea dry-heaved and slumped on the rim on the toilet. She hadn't been ill since she was a child. She was supposed to be strong. Nothing ruled her but Mother. Well, not anymore. Mother was dead, and whatever was inside of her body, it chained her to the commode.

"I wish the H.S.P.C. had killed me," she groaned. "I don't even believe in wishes or prayer, but oh God, I'm praying for death."

"Don't say that, Tea-cup. This'll pass. It's withdrawal from the drugs." Baron's hands stroked back her hair. Tea must look like she had gone on a drinking binge the night before.

Disorientated, she leaned her head back on Baron's thighs. She gripped his pants until her knuckles turned white. Time stood still. She had no idea how long she'd been sick.

"You should probably sip water." Her hands trembled as Duke handed her a glass. She only managed to wet her lips. She held the cup out. It wavered and began to slip from her fingers. Baron caught the bottom and handed the glass to his brother.

"I'll help you." Baron lifted her into his arms. Her head spun. Tea closed her eyes as she gripped his thick shoulders.

"I want off this ride," she groaned. "Kill me."

"Shush, little Tea." Duke ran his fingers through her hair. "We're not going to kill you, and you're not going to kill us. We're taking care of you."

"Do you want an IV?" Baron asked. "Say the word."

"No needles."

"No needles." One of the twins agreed as they left the bathroom.

When she opened her eyes again, she was still snuggled in Baron's arms, but he stood next to his bed. Her whole body felt ice cold.

"I never thought I'd freeze to death, but God is a cold-blooded bastard. I shouldn't be surprised."

"You're not going to freeze to death." Baron squeezed her to his chest as he knelt on the bed. "Get under the blanket."

"Take that, God. Still not dead." Tea slipped against the soft sheets. "Bring it on." The robe she wore puffed up and slapped her face. One of the twins pushed the terrycloth downward.

"Shush, Tea-cup." Baron sat at the foot of the mattress and slipped off his shirt. Duke paced near her shoulder.

"What are you doing?" Duke asked when he spotted his brother's naked torso. His eyes slanted into a glare.

"I've been reading about hypothermia in my book. It's exactly like if we pulled her out of a snowbank. Mather said to warm her." Baron stood up and dropped his pants. He wore loose gray boxer shorts. "I'm going to use body heat to bring her temp up."

"We need to think about this." Duke picked up a yo-yo and tossed it up and down. "It's probably too personal."

"If we sit around thinking, she's going to get colder." Baron flipped the blanket back and slipped into the bed next to her.

Tea gravitated toward the radiating heat.

"I don't want to take her to the hospital, do you? I don't know what else to do that might work."

"No. I want Tea here." Duke's eyes jumped to her.

She couldn't talk right now. Her teeth chattered. She didn't mind Baron in bed with her. All she could do was shake like a Chihuahua anyway.

"I want her here, too."

"I shouldn't have to fight an iguana for my electric blanket." Duke set his yo-yo on the dresser.

Under the blanket, Tea slipped out of the robe and turned. Baron's warm, naked chest pressed into her back as she snuggled closer to the human fireball. The cotton of his underwear brushed against her ass. As much as the lack of clothing wasn't safe, she did admit to herself that the heat beckoned. She pushed harder as if she could absorb the warmth. She wanted to give God the finger.

"You could help." Baron's voice snapped above her head. "With two of us, this might go faster."

Duke paced at the foot of the bed. He shoved his hands into his pockets as he watched his brother. Tea followed him with her eyes, but after the third pass, the movement made her stomach roll.

"This doesn't seem right." Even though Duke's statement sounded like he wasn't on board, his hands went to his shirt. "What about a hot bath?"

"The water will get too cold too fast." Baron wrapped an arm around her waist.

"Come here, Duke." Tea trembled. She needed the body heat. Some part of her whispered that she would never be warm again.

"For the love of Pete, hurry up, bro. This is like holding an ever-loving snowman."

Closing her eyes, Tea pictured a snowman melting as her head twirled and her stomach spasmed. Tea's hair was brushed to the side and a hand settled on her shoulder. Gentle petting like this made her sure she was stoned off her ass.

"Telling me I'm going to hold a snowman doesn't make me want to do this, dude." When Tea's eyes opened, Duke wore loose black shorts that hung on his hips. They looked like they might fall off at any moment. The roped muscles of his chest and arms made her salivate.

"Just get in," Baron grumbled.

When Duke lifted the blankets, cold air wafted and chilled her.

"This is probably a little too personal." Duke's huge, meaty hands wrapped around her waist. His palms branded her with fire. She needed heat, and they had it.

Baron's voice rumbled behind her. "A little while to keep her warm and I'll keep checking her temp. When she stabilizes, then we can go."

"Come here, little Tea." Duke pulled her to his chest and sucked in a sharp breath. "Where is her robe?" He exclaimed when skin met skin.

"She shook it off."

"My nipples could cut glass," Duke gasped. "Thanks for the heads up."

"I think my dick froze off ten minutes ago." Baron laughed. "I'm not going to ask you to strip the wire later."

"What do you mean?" Tea's teeth chattered.

"I'll let that one go." Baron laughed.

"Strip the wire?" She inhaled as warmth hugged her. The toasty heat was fantastic.

"Forget it," Duke muttered.

Tea closed her eyes and buried her face in the nook of Duke's neck. He smelled like metal and yummy man. If she was dying, then holding this man with the other twin at her back was the way to go.

"Am I going to die?" For the first time in her life, she considered that this might be her real end. She would die still angry at life, fuming at God, and pissed at herself. She didn't want that.

"We won't let you." Baron's breath was warm on her shoulder.

"Are you keeping me alive so that you can use me? I can't do anything for you. You'd be wasting your time."

"Nothing about you is a waste of time. We'll never hurt you, Tea. Anything we do is to help you," Baron insisted.

"You'll see. Everyone uses me sooner than later. There is no *loving compassion*. There is no help. There is only what you want and what you'll do to me." That Luna woman was out of her mind. Forgiveness, love, peace— she didn't have any of those things. Tea had nothing.

"That's probably not true, little Tea." Duke was as adamant as his brother. She lifted her head. His eyes glimmered like deep freshly cracked glacial ice, but there was a heat there. And trust. How could they both be so naïve? She'd lived with Mother. Tea knew things.

"Probably? No, it's true. I know how life works. Don't let my age fool you."

"You're age?" Baron asked.

"Just because I'm only twenty doesn't mean I don't know how the world works. I've lived on a harvester train as a slave for two years. I've seen the kind of dark things that haunt people's nightmares. You'll say you want to 'help' me. But there are conditions and strings attached. It's all a game we're playing."

"Who slit your throat?" Duke's voice was a mere whisper.

"You can't ask her that," Baron groaned.

"Why not?"

"Because she's sick. Doctor Mather said she might be more candid than normal. It would be the drugs talking. Actually, he said you might say something I don't want to hear, but that's shit, bro. We're going to talk about you being unhappy after Tea is stable."

Tea's dizziness returned, and her hands tingled. She pressed her palms to the abs in front of her to stabilize the crazy spinning in her head. Her fingers traced the muscles.

"I'm not going to talk to you." Tea slipped her hand up Duke's abs and then tucked her cold hands under his arms. He hissed. After a few minutes, she changed her mind. "Maybe I don't care anymore. I'm dying, right?" She chuckled to herself. "What's more fitting than at the end, I tell you about the beginning?"

"Tea, you don't have to." Baron ran his hand up and down her spine.

"Are you saying she won't lie—" Duke began.

"No, I want to tell you." She interrupted Duke. If they knew, then they wouldn't be such guileless goobers. "My grandma's boyfriend cut my throat when I was eighteen."

She'd never said the words out loud before. Not even to Mother. Telling the past wasn't as horrible as she thought it would be. She would tell the truth for the first time. The confession was like opening her baggage and tossing the items to the wind. She didn't want to carry that around with her anymore, especially as she headed into the afterlife. Sharing her past horror freed her. Somewhere along the way, Tea thought saying the words would open up the wound and she would bleed out.

"Tea." Baron exhaled her name like a prayer. Her name on his lips was more of a comfort than anything else that could've been said.

"My drugged-out mom didn't want me or my sister, Teresa. She dumped us with my crazy religious grandma when I was eight and Teresa was six, so she could go back to the Party Base. My grandma hated us. She used us and beat us. If we wanted food, we had to weave fabric bags that she sold along the train platform. She kept us like animals." Tea ran her hand over the scar on her throat. Now that she said what happened, it all seemed easier. What happened to her was merely the past. The past couldn't hold her anymore. No one could hold her. She was on her own now.

"Tea-cup, you don't have to—"

"—tell us, if you don't want to."

Tea ignored the twins and kept talking. "When I was eighteen, I planned my getaway, but my sister wouldn't go. I didn't know why. I begged her. I couldn't leave Teresa. My sister wasn't that smart. She was weak and younger than me. She needed me." Tea turned around and faced Baron. Her head dropped to his solid chest. She listened to Baron's strong heartbeat. "One night, I figured out why Teresa wouldn't leave. My grandma's boyfriend was sleeping with Teresa. His name was Warren. Warren had convinced my sister that he loved her. He told her he was going to marry her, even though he was in his fifties and she was only sixteen. It was sickening how he manipulated her. My sister was so inexperienced. We both were." Tea gulped back the tears that clogged her throat. "I was so naive." She gulped again. "When Teresa wouldn't listen to me, I did something I shouldn't have done. I told my grandma about the relationship thinking she would get rid of Warren. It didn't go like I thought."

"Tea, you don't have to tell us this," Baron reminded her.

"You said you didn't want to talk," Duke added.

She shook her head. Yes, she did. She had to tell someone before she died.

"My grandmother confronted Warren. I was there claiming that I would tell the H.S.P.C. how he had brainwashed my little sister. So brave and so reckless. I called him a disgusting pig for having sex with a sixteen-year-old." The memory flooded her brain. She'd been trying most of her life to forget what happened, but she never could. She'd never been able to let it go. At this moment with the twins, facing her death, she wanted to put the memory to rest. "That's when it all turned."

"Shush, Tea. We're going to help you." Baron rocked into her, and Duke cradled her head. The heat and strength radiating off these two men lulled her. The tears subsided. She absorbed their quiet stability.

"I hated him. I hated how he convinced her. He used Teresa. She didn't understand what was going on." Tea reminded herself that the long-ago time in her life was over, except the past never seemed to be over. That last night, the last time he touched her sister, it had changed her world forever.

"I don't get—" Duke rumbled behind her.

"—why he would do it?" Baron asked.

"When grandma and I forced the issue, he turned on us like a crazy person." She closed her eyes. She could still see him, furious and screaming. "When grandma and I went to him, we said they had to break up, or we'd tell the H.S.P.C. That's when I found out. What I didn't know at the time was that *he* was an agent. Gram's boyfriend was a respected H.S.P.C. agent. Warren decided to kill grandma and me, so we'd never tell. He said he would keep Teresa, and there was nothing we could do about it."

"I'm so sorry, little Tea." Duke's breath was a wisp of air on her shoulders.

"I survived. I gained my gift that night. Agent Warren killed my grandma and then went after me. He cut my throat, but in the end, I killed him instead. My sister ran. She was so scared. Teresa was sure we'd be in trouble for killing an H.S.P.C. agent. She felt responsible since she was the one who'd been sleeping with him. After the agent was dead, I left with a bandage around my throat. I wrapped it all by myself. No one will 'help' you." Tea considered the fact that killing that one agent had changed her whole life.

"You can rely on us, Tea-cup," Baron murmured into her hair. "Self-defense at the age of eighteen is brave. Now go to sleep. We'll be here to help you when you wake up."

"Don't you want to know about all the other people I killed too?" She should explain all the inexcusable things she'd done for Mother. Once they understood, they would hate her. That's how this would go. The twins *should* hate her. They should be her adversaries. They shouldn't hold her and forgive her. Enemies were all she'd ever had.

Duke pressed closer. He kept the cold at bay. "We'll listen if you want to talk."

"Will you feel better if you tell us?" Baron asked.

"No, I won't feel better," she whispered. "But I want you to know." More heat infused her. "I was on a harvester train searching for my sister when I met Mother. Mother was with The Originals and had a growing following of worshipers. She said she'd met Teresa and kept her. Mother promised to let me have my sister back if I did what she wanted. She said she would help me. I know now what it means when someone says that."

"What did she—" Duke started.

"—want from you?" Baron finished.

"She made me her slave." A sob escaped her when memories of Mother's cruelty flashed through her head. "I did every horrible thing she commanded me to do even if I didn't think it was right. Sometimes, Mother would put people in boxes and give them Snow Flu. I don't know how she did that, but I never stopped her. Instead, I helped her do insane things like that. Mother completely controlled me worse than my grandma did. She said I could have my sister if I did one more little thing. The requests went on and on. A week turned into a month, a month into a year. A year became two. I obeyed hoping and praying and wishing like a chump. I simply wanted Mother to give me my sister. I wanted to save her. Teresa needed me."

"Did Mother finally release your sister?" Baron caught a tear on her cheek with his thumb.

"Teresa was dead from the beginning. Mother killed her right after she met me. It was all a lie so Mother could control me and use my gift of strength," Tea whispered. "My sister wasn't smart, and she wasn't gifted. Mother didn't want to deal with her, and she couldn't use her. I found that out when the H.S.P.C finally captured us." Tea gulped down the tears clogging her throat. "All that, and Teresa was dead from the start. I was a sucker. That's what people do. They say they'll help you, but they use you."

"When you told the council this, they probably should've been lenient with you. You were—"

"—a slave trying to help your sister. I'd do anything for Duke. I know we fight, but I do care about him." Baron's eyes flipped to his brother.

"At the trial, no one would listen. I was Teagan, Mother's right hand. I was considered just as guilty, no matter my reasons. They didn't want to hear what I had to say. The world can go to hell. I know that the only options are to fight or die. Mother used me all the way up to the last moment I was with her." Tea gave a bitter laugh. Explaining depleted her remaining energy. There. She said it all. She could die in peace now. Tea slumped against the boy's warm bodies.

"I know you'd do anything for me," Duke whispered after a few moments. Tea started to drift off, but his declaration caught her attention. "I'm not still mad about what happened when Mom and Dad died, Baron."

"Are you unhappy here?"

"I don't know." Duke shifted and then ran his fingers through her hair.

Tea wondered if they were having another of those silent conversations, and then Baron's voice broke the hush that had fallen over them.

"I'd be pissed if you killed yourself."

Duke snorted. "I know." He paused. "Perhaps I felt lonely. You got Mather and work, I got…"

"You have me. I won't ditch you again." Baron shifted, and she felt the plastic thermometer on her forehead. "Say the word and we can move or have more people around. I know this is hard but I'm in it with you."

"I'm not into having a bunch of people around," Duke murmured. "I know who I am, but life started to feel empty. I can't explain it."

"We could go to a new base. People hate us because we fight, but we could work harder at that. I'm trying not to hit you as much. Do you want friends? We can ask for a place that isn't hidden in the back if we stop brawling."

"No. It's probably not the place or the friends." Duke sighed. "I want something more than this. I used to think about a wife or a home, but never mind. It's better now."

"Because of Tea?"

"Yes," Duke agreed.

"Tea-cup, are you awake?" Baron gave a hushed whisper. She didn't respond. Talking was too much work. She rolled over and pressed her butt back into Baron's crotch. He swore, and she snuggled in further, smiling.

"I like when she smiles." Duke played with a strand of her hair.

Silence fell between them, and the cloud in her brain grew. She could sleep for a while. When she got up, she would feel better, stronger. Once she was healthy, then she would plan her getaway or not, whichever.

"Duke?" Baron whispered. "Did you read this whole file?"

"No, most of it I don't understand. Why?"

"Look at this." She heard a rustle of paper, but she didn't open her eyes. She didn't care what was in that file. She'd lived it. "You might be even less lonely."

"Does inseminate mean what I think it does?"

"If you think it means pregnancy, you're right."

Chapter 8

Fabric held her down like a wimpy harvester was trying to strangle her from behind. She shoved until she was free of the blankets and sat up. Room, bed, robe, déjà vu. This was all like yesterday, or yesterday didn't even happen. Everything was misty. A vague memory.

As she shoved a wayward curl off her face, she recalled a bath then sleep. She had a dream of the twins' naked chests, smooth skin, and deep seductive voices. Odd, but sexy.

Did she have sex? Glancing down at her body, she didn't think so. A big fluffy robe engulfed her skinny frame. Her bladder insisted she rise. Funny, but she could've sworn she'd done all this before.

Tea hurried to the bathroom. After relieving herself, she stared in the mirror. Her hair was shorter and brushed. She opened the drawer and found a pair of scissors. Yes, she'd cut her hair and then tried to kill Duke. If she had held scissors to one of the twins' jugulars, she wouldn't still be in one of their beds. No one was *that* forgiving. They would've called the H.S.P.C. Unless that was all a dream.

Returning to the bedroom, Tea decided she should go back to bed. Her stomach growled. No. She needed to eat to get stronger. Tea made up her mind she would play this "being nice" game for a few days.

Tea gripped the door handle as she peeked out into the apartment. At first glance, she thought the room was empty. The exit was straight ahead of her. She could sneak out. Her eyes zeroed in on that option. Once she was free, she could...

Tea stepped into the living room. What could she do? Where would she go?

Just as Tea was about to slap herself for her own indecision, she spotted Duke. The older twin crouched next to the dining table by the door. A long fat metal tube was partly assembled on the wide wooden surface. She recognized the tube as a battery that the smaller shuttles used. Wires stuck up everywhere in front of Duke's face. He stood up with a soldering iron in his hands, but appeared to be completely engrossed in his work.

For some reason, Tea could see variations in the twins. She didn't know why, but Duke looked different to her than Baron. Duke took three steps back from the table as he seemed to study his work. When he stopped, he directly blocked the front door. He used the back of his wrist to push plastic goggles into his hair. He scratched his head as he stared at the wires. Around his feet, ash and metal shavings dusted the floor.

Tea shrugged. She would have to make this up as she went along. The only thing she knew was that she couldn't stay here forever. If she stayed, then these men would control her. Everyone turned against her sooner or later.

Inching out of the bedroom door, she spotted Baron. The younger twin moved around the L-shaped kitchen carrying a dented watering can. Tea didn't notice it before, but beyond the counter was a square cove of plants. Above the mini garden was a bright LED screen mimicking a sunny day. The light made the green plants look like plastic, but the mock sunshine lit up Baron's face. He grinned as he watered an overgrown pot of Rosemary.

When he set the watering container down, he glanced up at her. Their eyes locked.

"You look so much better, Tea-cup." His face split into a wide, toothy grin. "Not so pale." He bounded over to her and pulled out that damn thermometer from his pocket. This time, Tea was resigned when he ran the tip across her forehead.

As soon as Baron spoke Tea's nickname, Duke lifted his head away from the wires. He tossed the tools and the goggles on the table and then joined his brother next to her. He stared as he shoved his hands in his pockets. When he caught her eye, he tugged her into his arms and hugged her. She thought about fighting him but didn't. Her stomach flip-flopped. The flutter must be her hunger.

"I was worried about you. I got scared that perhaps you wouldn't wake up." Duke's hands returned to his pockets.

"I told you not to worry. It's bad for your health." Baron hugged her next. She tensed under the feel of their welcoming embrace. They needed to stop being friendly right this instant.

"You were worried? What do you mean?" Her eyes narrowed. He should feel relieved if she was no longer a bother.

"I mean, I was worried. Are you feeling well?" Duke frowned.

"Feeling well?" she repeated. "Why do you care?"

"Because we like you." Baron smiled.

"You like me?" Tea refrained from asking what the hell that meant.

"Did you throw up again?" Duke asked.

"Damn." Tea's eyebrows rose. She thought that was a dream. Her cheeks heated under their intense gazes.

Duke shoved Baron. "Perhaps we shouldn't talk about that now."

"Perhaps." Tea rolled her eyes. "Probably."

Baron tugged on her hand. "Doctor Mather made applesauce. Come and eat, Tea-cup."

"His applesauce tastes like an apple puked," Duke whispered to her.

"No, it doesn't." Baron tugged on her arm.

"I think your taste buds are broken." Duke punched Baron's arm.

"I feel like we've had this conversation before." Baron let go of her hand and pushed Duke.

"We've had *all* the conversations before," Duke snapped as he raised his fist.

"You don't have to eat it. Tea does. She's the one that's—"

"Timeout. I'm not hungry." Tea interrupted the bourgeoning argument. Telling her the food was apple puke wasn't the most appetizing description. Hunger was better. Her stomach growled. No. Not better. "Damn, I am hungry."

"Ha." Baron took her hand again and tugged her into the kitchen. Duke hurried ahead of her and pulled out a broken stool that looked like the seat was glued back together with excessive amounts of adhesive. Tea followed Baron over to the counter and perched on the cushion while he filled a small bowl of mush from the fridge.

"This doesn't taste the best, but if you're feeding two, then you have to eat." Baron set the bowl in front of her and then handed her a spoon. "Pipe down, Duke. I don't need to hear your bull."

"Feeding two?" The spoon dropped from Tea's fingers and clattered onto the counter. That's what bothered her. Her eyes jumped back and forth. "Inseminate" was the last word her foggy memory recalled. *Damn*, she had told the twins practically her whole life story last night. She squinted at them.

"What's that look for?" Baron asked.

"If it's about the baby—" Duke began.

"No." Tea interrupted. "I tried to kill Duke. What the hell is wrong with you? Last night might've been the most fucked up evening I've ever had, and I've seen things that would make a hardened agent faint."

"Killed me with dull scissors." Duke picked up the spoon. "Cute."

"Ha," Baron smirked. "If you'd cut up his face, it would've been an improvement."

"You asked me about my life. I told you about being a slave." Tea closed her eyes and rubbed the scar on her neck. How could she make this un-happen?

"You volunteered the information."

When she opened her eyes, Baron held the spoon out to her.

"We told you that you didn't have to say anything." Duke shoved his hands into his pockets.

"I'm pregnant?" Somewhere that woman Tea had left on the tracks was laughing at her. Her eyes flew to the two men next to her. She was strong once, but she wasn't a force that could take on the world anymore. She was also traveling solo. Weak and alone. Her eyes jumped to the door.

"Don't panic, Tea. We'll help you." Duke took the spoon from Baron and placed the utensil in her hand. She wrapped her fingers around the metal handle like a lifeline.

"What do you mean by that?"

Duke leaned his forearms on the counter next to her. "Why do you—"

"—ask us that all the time?" Baron finished.

"Why do you keep saying you're here to help me? You don't even know me. What do you want?" It was driving her crazy. "What's the angle? What's the game?"

"Game?" Baron looked to his brother.

"No angle. We don't want anything." Duke gave a curt nod. "We simply want to help. In fact, say the word, and we're on it."

"There's no game. It's us with you." Baron pushed the bowl closer to her.

They were here now, being helpful, but what about in a few days, a few weeks, a year? And why did they keep saying "help" as if she needed them? She didn't need anyone. She would take care of herself and a baby. She was on her own exactly like Mother had said.

As her eyes jumped back and forth between the two huge men, her palm went to her belly. She would have to stay here at least until she gave birth. Without her gift, she couldn't protect the child. She also didn't know how to deliver a baby. She would need a doctor. Her eyes flipped to Baron. Close enough.

Was hiding here until she had the kid the best idea? She didn't have a lot of choices. Unfortunately, escaping was out.

"Are you upset that you don't know who the father is?" Baron asked when she sat in silence for so long.

"No." And she wasn't. Who the sperm donor was didn't matter to her in the least. "This will be my child."

"He was probably gifted, whoever the donor was." Duke shoved his hands in his pockets. "I've heard making more babies is something the H.S.P.C. does. Healthy women who are willing. I thought it was on a volunteer basis. I never heard of them impregnating a prisoner."

"How many prisoners have you met?" Baron punched his brother. "The guy just gave a sperm sample."

"I don't care who he is. The baby is mine. I'll protect it."

When Tea was a little girl, she made the promise that if she ever got pregnant, she would keep the baby and raise it and love it. She would be there. Not like her unfeeling parent, or her nonexistent father. She wouldn't be like her evil grandma either. Tea would love this baby the way no one ever loved her.

"I get that you probably have no reason to trust us or—" Duke began.

"—believe us, but we're here to help you," Baron finished. "I don't have any other way to say it. Don't ask us what we mean. When you're ready to leave you can, you're not a prisoner Tea, but—"

"—you need food, a place to sleep, and care. We're offering you that. No strings attached."

All her plans to run the first chance she got changed in an instant. She would protect this kid. She also might not know how to look after a baby, but she could learn. Her new plan was to stay here—for at least nine months.

"I can stay until the baby is born?" She spoke softly, but both the twins nodded.

"Stay for as long as you want and—"

"—we'll look after you. All you have to do is say the word."

She would have to believe them until they proved otherwise. As much as she didn't know why they would want to be so benevolent, she would have to trust them for now. She could make nine months. She'd managed to survive Mother's constant rule for years. Nine months was nothing.

"What if the H.S.P.C. comes for me? For us?" She swirled the apple mush. "You're taking a risk, a big one." She owed them. She supposed she should be used to servitude by now.

Baron snorted. "Like if an agent shows up here asking for the pregnant zombie cadaver that they sent us?"

"That's probably not going to happen. We can't even get a couple of bedframes," Duke scoffed. "We're hidden in the back of Water Base Cure. We tend to brawl. I don't know if you noticed the broken furniture. We also don't have any friends because we—"

"—fight all the time. People, agents, co-workers all say we're hard to deal with." Baron pulled the dried meat out of the fridge and set the package on the counter. "They get tired of us. We've hurt some guys on accident."

"And that one lady," Duke added.

"Chances are good that—"

"—probably no one is coming." Duke filled a cup with water and set the glass next to her.

"But we're going to keep you safe. We'll fight less so that you'll not get hurt. Don't worry. It's bad for your health." Baron smiled.

They had no reason to be this generous. She'd done nothing for them. They didn't trade favors. She studied their honest expressions and their glorious blue eyes. What did they want in exchange?

"You're serious, aren't you?" As much as she didn't know what the game was, they did seem sincere. They would hide her. She didn't know if that meant being a slave like with Mother or being a laborer like with her grandma, but it didn't matter either way. She would do whatever for her baby.

"As serious as we can be in a conversation that contains the words 'pregnant zombie cadaver' in it." Duke deadpanned.

"Ha." A smile tugged at Baron's lips. "Stay here with us, and if you want or need something, say the word."

"What am I supposed to do here?" Now they would tell her what the exchange was. Sex, maybe? That wouldn't be a hardship. She could do that. It had been a while, but sex was like weaving fabric bags. After she got started, she would remember what to do.

"Eat. Drink water. Nap," Baron rattled off. He pointed to her spoon, then gestured to the cup next to her.

"Nap?"

"And drink lots of water. You're dehydrated, and if you don't, I'll give you an IV. I know you hate needles, but I'll do it."

Tea's eyes widened in disbelief. "Drink water?" she sighed. "What am I supposed to do in exchange for you and your brother hiding me?"

"Probably rest mostly." Duke shrugged. "Let us help you."

Baron leaned over and kissed the tip of her nose. "Eat, drink water, nap," he repeated.

She supposed she could do that. As insane of a request that it was.

Chapter 9

Duke and Baron shouted back and forth in the living room while Tea threw Baron's wet scrubs in the dryer. The hollering hit an ear-piercing decibel as she grabbed his medical textbook off the dresser. After she hung Duke's damp towel on the hanger mounted to the door, she started for the screaming match.

Tea dashed around the two men roaring at each other and headed to the kitchen. Her guess, the towel issue started this particular battle.

"I don't want a wet towel in a ball on the floor. Use your own," Duke barked. "You've no respect for my stuff."

"Respect?" Baron sneered. "You took all my scrubs out of the washing machine to toss in your clothes. I need my scrubs clean. I have to go to work."

Tea grabbed a hunk of meat out of the fridge and then climbed onto the kitchen counter. She crawled to the middle, tucked her legs under her, and flipped open Baron's book to the cardiovascular system. Last night over dinner, Baron mentioned that Doctor Mather would be testing him on this chapter.

The shouting continued, but in the last three weeks, Tea had gotten proficient at tuning out the noise. The yelling didn't bother her. The hollering reminded her a little of the harvesters. As she ripped off a hunk of meat, she noted Baron threw the first punch this time. Last time, it was Duke who struck when Baron wasn't ready.

As Baron attacked his brother, Duke wrapped his arms around the other man's waist and flipped him to the floor.

Tea cringed and then went back to eating. She kept an eye on the bout as she snacked and scanned pages. She underlined a few of the things Doctor Mather would be testing Baron on today.

When Duke grasped a screwdriver, Tea put two fingers in her mouth and gave out a whistle that could silence an entire harvester train. Both men grabbed their ears and rolled in pain. The screwdriver clattered to the floor.

"Timeout. No weapons. Baron has to go to work." Tea held up her hand.

"Tea-cup." Baron stood. "What're you doing sitting in the middle of the counter?"

"Eating where I won't get knocked over." Tea slipped to the edge of the marble and then dropped to the floor.

"We're sorry, little Tea." Duke came to his feet and stretched his neck back and forth. "Outstanding, Baron. We make her eat on the counter."

"I don't care." Tea closed the book and slipped the notecards out of the back. "I've eaten in worse places." She handed the cards to Baron. "I made you study cards for your test."

"You did?" Baron took the papers and stared at them as if they might start a fire.

"I threw your damp clothes in the dryer, but you have an extra set of scrubs on the back of the door in the bathroom." As she spoke, she picked up a forgotten bowl of applesauce. One of the boys must have left it out. She slipped the dish back into the fridge. "You should get ready for work."

"Right, work." Baron's brow wrinkled in confusion. He eyed his brother. Tea hated when the two of them had silent conversations. Sure, she didn't say a lot, but it wasn't like she was telling secrets. She was simply keeping to herself for self-preservation.

"Duke." Tea grabbed a pack of ice from the freezer and handed the plastic sack to the older twin. "This is for your neck." Her eyes jumped to where his hands still rubbed his collar bones. "And I hung up your towel."

"Oh, yeah, my towel." Duke held the ice to the side of his neck as he shoved his other hand into his pocket. The pocket thing was a type of uncomfortable gesture when he was trying to think. Same with his "probably" and "perhaps" with every breath he took.

So far, things seemed alright. Tea had learned how to read the twins well enough to manage. Now if she could only figure out how to ask for what she wanted. Two issues crept up she wanted changed. Tea still weighed the risks. Every time she'd ever said anything, there was always a punishment.

"I have to head to work," Baron muttered.

"Me too." Duke stuffed his hand in his pocket as he headed over to his work table. She figured he must be hung up on a problem.

After a few minutes, Tea followed Baron into the bedroom. For the last three weeks, she often got up early with him and Duke. This part of the day was her favorite. She liked to sit by the bathroom door and watch him shave. She didn't know why the mundane activity fascinated her, but watching the razor never failed to charm her as his hands slowly moved over his face.

Since she was working up the courage to talk to one of the twins about what she did here, she took a few minutes to collect her thoughts.

As Baron filled the sink with water, she considered what she wanted to say to the younger twin. Talking to both men was a challenge. The boys made her question everything she thought she knew. Duke didn't say much unless it was the middle of the night when Baron was asleep. He stayed bent over his batteries most days, and Baron was always at the hospital. Even though past lessons dictated speaking up was never a good idea, she made up her mind.

At first, she thought to eat, drink water, and nap wasn't a bad exchange, but now she was going out of her mind. Especially since the twins only minorly paid attention to her. They had a strict schedule that never varied even with her introduction.

First, it was morning hygiene rituals. After that they worked all day. In the evenings, the twins did yoga, ate dinner, and then slept. The only action that ever interrupted their routine was fighting. Then again, even their boxing matches had become predictable. She could see a battle coming a mile away. But Tea was done being a ghost watching them live their lives.

That brought her to now. She had to repay them for hiding her and the baby. And Tea couldn't just keep sitting. Even though she didn't have her gift, she must have something they wanted. She needed the twins to need her.

Creeping closer to the bathroom door, Tea stopped and took a deep breath. Baron hadn't shut the door all the way. The light flicked from the slight opening. She peeked in and stared at Baron's shirtless back. The muscles flexed under his skin as he shaved his face. He brought his hands up. The razor started at his neck, then slipped past his chin.

After a few seconds, her eyes dropped to his loose shorts and the way the fabric hung off his sculpted ass. She'd seen him do this often, and it never failed to turn her on. Rarely, did Baron notice her observing his routine. These were the only movements she let herself fantasize about sex with the twins.

"You should nap."

Tea jumped. Her eyes flipped to Baron's more cobalt blue gems in the mirror. She hated the word *nap*.

"It's morning. I just got up," she pointed out.

"Ha." Baron smiled at her in the mirror and then patted the flat part of the counter next to the sink.

The offer to disrupt his activity stunned her. It was a pleasant surprise that he gave her an opening.

"Can I talk to you now?" Tea tightened her grip on the belt of her fluffy robe. "What about work?"

"You can always talk to Duke or me." He resumed shaving. "Don't worry."

"I know it's bad for my health." She entered the room.

"I was going to say don't worry. Doctor Mather is always late for work." He paused. "What can I do for you, Tea-cup?"

Tea hopped up on the counter. "You said if I wanted or needed something all I had to do was say the word."

"Nothing wrong with your memory." As he stared at his reflection, she studied his profile. Both twins were so attractive that some days it was hard to believe that they were real. Besides the charming smiles, the striking blue eyes, and the muscles, the twins were kindhearted. They kept saying all they wanted was to help her, and she still didn't find the angle. Spending time with them was like hanging out with a couple of unicorns.

"Are you sick?" Baron paused with his razor. "I should get a urine sample. I'll do that tonight."

That comment spurred her into action. This was exactly one of her issues. She couldn't handle being coddled like a sick patient anymore. Never in her life had she spent so much time loafing. She had the overwhelming need to do something to repay the twins for their generosity. Never had she wanted to give or be kind to someone other than her sister, but now the idea ruled her.

"I wanted to talk to you about doing something."

"Like?"

Tea took a breath. First, she would fix the food. She was sick of eating dried meat and applesauce. Duke was right. The sauce tasted like an apple vomited into a bowl. Last week, when she asked about their diet, the boys admitted that they couldn't cook. Well, she could cook *something* edible. Cooking would be handy for the baby. She was sure of it.

"I want to cook." She didn't add that she didn't know how. She would share that information once she got started, or never. Whichever.

"No."

The "no" was so swift that the sharp response shocked her. What was wrong with cooking? They had a kitchen, and she couldn't sit on the sofa indefinitely. Already she was certain her ass print would be there for years to come. What happened to their "say the word" credo?

"But you said—"

"No, Tea." He cut her off. "You already do our laundry, fix furniture, pick up and…" His eyes dropped to the counter where the note cards for his test sat. He slipped the cards into the pocket of his shorts. "Nap."

A scowl blanked her features. First, her grandma used her to weave fabric bags all day long for sale along the tracks, and then she was a slave to Mother's every whim. But this wasn't really a better spot. The twins only wanted her to sit like a statue, or a trinket, or a teacup. Again, she was under someone's thumb. This time she wasn't going to accept someone else's dictate. She should be allowed to return the favor. If she had nine months of this sloth-like existence, she would choke them, and it had nothing to do with escaping. It would be on pure principle.

"Don't look at me like that." Baron patted his clean-shaven face with a towel and then set the cloth next to her.

"You don't understand." Tea stared at the floor and gripped the edge of the counter.

Baron tipped her chin upward. She expected him to kiss the tip of her nose like he always did.

For the last three weeks, Baron would remind her to eat, drink water, and nap. After he gave her his list, he would kiss the tip of her nose before he would go off and either do yoga with Duke, head to work, or go to sleep. She was starting to hate the brotherly gesture as much as the word "nap."

"*You* don't understand," he murmured. "We're helping you, and you don't have to do anything in return." His breath was warm, and she felt his exhale fan her cheeks. "We're keeping you safe."

He leaned in and before he reached her nose, she tilted her head. His mouth landed on hers. Tea had dreamt about his lips and couldn't pass up this one little touch. This might be a bad idea, but once his mouth was on hers, nothing mattered, only his taste. She sighed as their breaths mingled.

As soon as her lips parted, his tongue speared in with unexpected urgency. At first, Baron was aggressive like he was impatient. The twins were always patient with her, but she did note that Baron had the proclivity to jump headfirst into things. The only time they lost their temper was with each other, but his tongue slipped into her mouth as if demanding entrance. Baron was diving in, and she loved it. Their tongues dueled as his arms roughly pulled her closer to his chest. He tasted like mint and an essence that was all Baron.

Baron's abrupt reaction thrilled her. His pelvis pushed against the counter, and she scooted forward to cuddle his growing erection. The heat of his shaft had a pulsating need that she could feel through the fabric of his shorts. She'd never felt this kind of mounting passion. The pressure of his length seared her inner thigh as her robe parted. His right hand slipped inside the terrycloth to steal around her waist. With his left hand, Baron brushed the underside of her breasts.

If they didn't let her cook, they could do this instead.

Tea moaned into his mouth as Baron used both hands to push the robe further apart. His hands traveled upward to her breasts as his fingers slipped over the stretchy fabric bra. Under the light covering, her nipples awoke. Her back arched into his hands.

"I fucking burned myself, pinhead." Duke's words came from the doorway. "You didn't think that one through. Outstanding. What now? Huh?"

Baron shoved away from Tea like she'd contacted Snow Flu. He stumbled backward then stumbled out of the bathroom doorway. She thought she heard him mumble "For the love of Pete" and "work," but the rest of what he might've said was undecipherable. She pulled her robe closed and stared in shock. What just happened? As fast as the kiss happened, it un-happened.

"Out." Duke gave the sharp order and pointed to the door with his thumb. He held his hand with a long, angry red mark. He moved to the sink, turned the lever for cold water, and then put his hand under the spout. "Out," he repeated. It wasn't that he yelled. The instruction was stern, but he might as well have yelled for how the one word made her flinch.

Tea slipped off the counter and hurried past him. She felt like a naughty child or a dog who had chewed the bathmat. Duke was clearly annoyed although she didn't understand exactly why. Tea should say something, she guessed. She was good at fake apologies, but an honest sorry she'd never done before.

Tea stared at the closed bathroom door. She wasn't sorry.

Back in the bedroom, she glanced around for Baron. She still needed to talk to him. Now more than ever. He must've taken his clothes with him. No one could dress that fast. She went to the dresser and pulled on a pair of Duke's sweatpants and hooded sweatshirt as she waited for the other twin.

Talking didn't go well. Not only did she not get a change in her routine, but the kiss had made their odd relationship even more awkward. Tea supposed she should regret his mouth on hers, but she didn't. That was one of the sweetest and hottest kisses she'd ever received. Being kissed was rare. In her sexual experience, most of the men Mother made her have sex with just did the basic in and out. Tea didn't even know people could kiss the way Baron did. She also supposed his mouth would be the best part of her day. From here on out, the most interesting thing she would do is make a deeper ass mark on the couch.

When the door to the bathroom opened, Tea spun around. As Duke headed to the closet, he scrubbed his wet face with his shirt. He didn't look at her. She had no idea what the rules were any more or what game they were even playing.

"I'm not sure if you're mad at me for kissing Baron, or if you're mad because you burned your hand," she sputtered out.

"What?" Duke pulled on a green shirt and then headed to the door.

"I'm not going to talk to you about it." She trailed after him. When they reached the living room, she exhaled her annoyance. "It's only that I'd say that the silence means you're angry. But since you rarely talk to me, I don't know if you're in your normal mood."

"I talk to you." Duke opened the fridge and then took out meat and popped the hunk into his mouth. "At night when you have nightmares, I sit with you. I probably talk more to you than anyone I've ever known."

"Probably? Perhaps?" His comment made her guffaw. "Duke, when you come into the room at night, I do all the talking."

Duke grinned at her. "You always start by saying you're not going to talk to me."

That was true. For some reason, as soon as she made up her mind not to share with the boys, and not to get deeper into this weird relationship, that's when words gushed out.

Tea wandered over to the couch and sat. "I'm not going to talk to you," she announced. "If you're mad I kissed Baron, then fine. Be mad."

Duke smirked at her, then strolled over to his battery. He picked up his soldering iron and looked at her. He lifted one blond eyebrow.

Damn.

"When you hold me at night, you don't tell me about yourself. You don't tell me about you." Tea leaned over the back of the couch, and the words tumbled out of her just like in the middle of the night. "I do all the talking. You don't say anything. And you don't even like it when I mention that you come into the room to hold me."

"Is this you not talking?" Duke grinned.

"Never mind." She slumped down on the couch and picked up her new best friend, a throw pillow.

"It's probably too personal." The soldering iron clattered to the table.

"If it's too personal to hold me, then why do you do it? If you don't want to hold me, don't." Tea sat up again and met his eyes.

"I said it's probably personal. I never said I didn't want to hold you. Besides, Baron needs his sleep. He has to be awake and focused in surgery. Just like I need not to get distracted when I'm working with the soldering iron." He glanced at the mark on his hand.

Tea rubbed the scar on her neck. "I'm trying to talk to you about Baron and me and living here." Tea knelt up on the couch. "I want to talk about our situation when we're awake. Not at night. Not after yoga, not while you're shaving. I want to do it here." She threw her arms out in a circle. "I want to talk now."

"Then do it." Duke bent over his battery and didn't look up. When she didn't speak right away, he did. "Can you hold this wire for a second?"

"Did you know that in the last three weeks, the only thing you've said to me is," she dropped her voice lower to mock him. "'Can you hold this wire?'" Tea shrugged. "I can't imagine you really need me to hold one little piece of wire."

Tea found it slightly comical that Duke didn't engage with her some other way. Whenever he asked his wire question, she thought he was checking to see if she was awake or asleep on the couch. Then she thought he was like an awkward teen who couldn't come up with anything better to say. She figured Duke liked to keep to himself. He was cautious when speaking with her. The sad part was… she looked forward to standing next to him holding a tiny wire. It was the highlight of her day. That and when she watched as they twisted into yoga positions.

"I'm not good at talking to women, but," Duke frowned at her, "if you don't want to hold it, say the word. I only asked because your hands are smaller than mine."

"You talk to me just fine." Tea cocked her head to the side. "Who told you that you aren't good at talking to women? Baron?"

"No." Duke stalked away from the battery and grabbed meat out of the fridge again. He popped it into his mouth before he shoved his hands in his pockets.

Tea frowned at the sharp one-word answer.

"Did Baron tell you not to help me anymore?" Duke asked suddenly. He looked like if his brother appeared right now, he would hit him.

"No, Baron didn't say anything," she explained quickly. "I just thought I wasn't helping you all that much." This morning when she rose, all she wanted to do was have a job other than nap, but she wasn't sure if this conversation was an improvement. "Are you mad at me for kissing Baron and this wire conversation is a way to not talk about it?"

"No." Duke bent over his battery again. He didn't ask a second time for her assistance. Tea supposed that was the end of their conversation, and that was fine with her. She wasn't sure she wanted to talk about any of this anyway.

"This just isn't working." Duke tossed a tool down.

"I know." Tea had to agree. So far, this strange living situation wasn't working. The twins never let her do anything, she was sick of napping, and she was attracted to both men. At least the temptation she could fight.

"What?" Duke's eyes popped to her in confusion. "No, I meant this wiring isn't working. I need two extra hands and smaller pliers."

Tea grinned. "Oh?"

"I'm not mad about Baron. I was surprised." Duke came around the table and offered her his hand. Tea took his outstretched fingers, and his warm palm pressed to hers. Yes, this was already a step up over the last few weeks of leisure. At least she wasn't being ignored.

"We can talk about it if it's bothering you." Duke didn't stop at the work table but headed to a door next to the broken bookshelf. She *assumed* the entrance was a storage closet like the one for brooms in the kitchen. A small part of her hesitated as he pulled her along.

"When my grandma was cross with Teresa and me, she would lock us in the closet until the devil let go of our souls." Tea tugged out of Duke's hand. "I'm a little too old to sit in a closet thinking about what I've done."

Duke stopped and turned to her.

"I'm probably never going to shove you into a closet, little Tea." Duke sighed. "I hope one day you'll trust Baron and me. I said I'm not mad at you."

"Are you mad at him? If you're mad, you should say it. Hell, I'm the first one to admit that saying what's on your mind isn't always the best. I've learned that the hard way." Tea rubbed the scar around her neck. "But this time, I'd like to know what you're thinking."

"For a woman who only talks to me when she's half asleep, that's cute." Duke opened the door and sailed through. "I'm not sure how to talk to a beautiful and complicated woman like you, Tea. I don't have a lot of practice, and I don't want to get it wrong."

Tea trailed along, and her eyes alighted on what was not a closet.

Chapter 10

The room she entered was long and narrow, but quite massive with high ceilings. On both sides sat dusty metal shelves filled with gadget and wires. A wall to her direct left had hooks from floor to ceiling. Overhead the lights above her hummed, and she could vaguely hear the trains not far off. The twins truly lived on the edge of the base.

As she glanced at the cement wall, she noted that above each hook was a label, but nothing hung from the pegs. Spools of wires littered the floor mixed with tools and documents. A train whistle blew, and she heard a muffled screech.

"I have to find needle-nose pliers." Duke hunted around the floor. "If you want to talk, I'll listen. I'm not upset with you, Tea. I'm not shoving you into a closet."

"Find pliers?" Tea glanced around. "In this mess, who could find anything? This room is as bad as your apartment."

"I know the place is broken." Duke's shoulders dropped. "It's not a place for a woman or children. I haven't gotten around to fixing all the furniture we've broken in our fights."

"I fixed the stool yesterday, but you both broke it this morning."

Duke shoved his hands in his pockets.

"We've been working hard on not brawling since you got here, but I swear the fighting takes us over. We don't want to start a fight and accidentally knock you over. You could lose the baby. I'm glad you've been sitting on the counter. I want you and the baby to be alright."

"What does that mean?"

"It means," Duke grinned at her and then bent over to pick up a hammer, "I like the idea of you and a kid being around. I could probably teach him to play catch or something like that. I can take him to the schoolroom in the morning."

"What if it's a girl?"

"Girls play catch and go to school too." Duke's eyes gleamed in amusement.

Tea stared for a moment. Duke thought of himself as a dad. She didn't know what to say. Instead of commenting, she began to walk around the workroom.

"What am I looking for?" She picked up a spool of wire and hung it. As she strolled, she put items away and scooped up papers.

"You're the one who wanted to talk. Talk." Duke appeared next to her and took a stack of files from her hands. "I'll find it. Sometimes it's not easy to switch the way I see things. Give me a minute."

Tea picked up a screwdriver then cocked her head. "The way you see things?"

"Sure." Duke's eyes flipped to hers. "You know how Baron can see cells?"

"Cells?" Tea picked up a small spool of yellow wire and placed it on the hook with the matching label.

"Baron is gifted with the ability to see microscopically. He told you that. Because of the gift, that's why he's a surgical assistant. He wasn't always in medicine," Duke scoffed. "He started after he found out he could see things like he's looking through a microscope. The other doctors don't have time for him. They think he's dumb."

"I've heard him say that before." At dinner, Baron mentioned that he felt he was lacking. His insecurity was one of the reasons she'd been helping him study. That, and she was desperate for something to do. She glanced at the scattered tools on the floor. "He sees cells. What do you see?"

"I see electricity." Duke crouched next to a tub of wire clippings. "I have to adjust my vision sometimes."

"That's why you fix batteries for the H.S.P.C. They are using your gift." Tea had wondered why Duke did this work. She gathered that he didn't love it. Baron didn't like the hospital, but she knew he was trapped into the work due to his gift. This made her understand Duke a little better.

"Yes. After my gift came in, I was dumped here to do this work. The electricity doesn't care what wire I pick, but the H.S.P.C. does. I have to do everything to their specifications." Duke straightened. "Here is the tool I need." He held up small pliers and then scanned her. "It's too messy for you in here. After I get this work done, you should rest. I won't ask for help anymore. Perhaps it's a bother. I should've considered that... probably."

"It wasn't bothering me." Tea struggled to pick up a spool of wire, but the bundle was too heavy. Duke appeared at her side and scooped the wires up with one hand. He placed the wheel in the labeled spot. "You should have someone to work with you."

"The H.S.P.C. gave me an assistant who worked with me in this stockroom. He told me what batteries I had to repair. He also kept the tools and wires organized and managed the log."

"Where is he?"

"When he met his match, he moved." Duke had a wistful tone to his voice. Tea studied the longing that swathed his face. Staring at his eyes, Tea wondered if Duke didn't care about her kissing Baron after all. He could prefer men. Duke sounded like he deeply missed his male assistant.

"You liked him?" she asked. "You like men?"

"No." Duke paused holding a set of goggles. He squinted at her as he hung them on a nail. "I mean, I liked his company, and he was a good worker, but not sexually. Why do people think that?"

"People?"

"I guess not people. You," he paused, "and Doctor Mather. I don't know why. I guess perhaps it's because Baron and I don't spend any time with women. That's probably for the best."

"I thought you might like guys because you sounded like you missed this assistant a little too much."

"I'm not into men. I…" He paused a second time and stared at the tools scattered over the floor. "I thought that perhaps by now we would've met our match. Someone to love us." Duke's words were so quiet that if she hadn't been listening so intently, she might've missed them. She recalled the conversation the night she was sick. Something about Doctor Mather thinking Duke would kill himself. The idea was frightening. She didn't want Duke depressed, but she didn't know how to comfort him. Tea was simply trying to come up with a way to not sit on the couch.

"You said you're lonely." She ran her hand along his arm. She wasn't practiced at giving solace. She might be unqualified, but she felt like she should say something. Duke and Baron always worked to make her happy. She tried to copy the things they did when they held her. "I remember."

"Nothing wrong with your memory." Duke chuckled. "It's okay, little Tea. I have you around now. I like your company. I'm not big on being around a bunch of people, never have, but having you around makes life better. And when the baby comes, I can help you with him or her. Don't worry about me. Baron says worry is bad for your health."

Tea sighed. If she wanted to worry about them, she would. They wouldn't be able to stop her. In the last three weeks, she had come to know them, and they had started to mean something to her. And their importance was more than them hiding her and the baby. She had to repay them.

Duke set the next spool of wire on the last hook before turning to the door. "After I solder one last piece, then I won't ask for anything else."

"You can ask me for help. I didn't mean that I wanted you to stop." Tea followed him back to the battery. "I want to be helpful to you or Baron and not be bored." The idea took shape, and she smiled. "I could organize your stockroom for you like your assistant did. What about that?"

"No." Duke's "no" was as fast as his brothers. Tea steamed as her hands curled into fists at her side. She held her temper. What was wrong with these two? She was trying to be cooperative. Couldn't they see she didn't know how else to repay them? Couldn't they see she was trying for the first time? She wasn't practiced at caring for anyone other than her sister, but they were real bastards to keep shooting her down.

"What do you mean?" Maybe she wasn't doing this properly.

"What do you mean, what do I mean? I mean no."

"No?"

"Eat, drink water and—"

"—nap," she finished. *Damn.* Now she finished his sentence like Baron did.

"Nothing wrong with your memory." Duke picked up the goggles he'd left on his worktable. He paused. "Can you hold this?"

Tea stepped in front of his table and arranged the two tiny wire pieces. After everything was to Duke's satisfaction, he set the tools to the side.

"This is good now."

When he stepped around her, Tea moved in front of him and stared stubbornly at his chest. She would make him understand.

"I want to do something for you. Anything. I thought you said I could ask. I thought all I had to do was say the word."

"You should probably talk to Baron." Duke took a slight step back. "I'm behind. I need to get back to work."

"And I could make it easier for you."

"No." He dropped his goggles over his eyes and wouldn't look at her. Tea wanted to scream.

She'd had it. Never had Tea bitten the hand that held her leash, but the urge to slap Duke bubbled to the surface. She threw her hands up and pressed them to his chest. If she'd had her strength, the action would've thrown Duke backward. As Tea was, her palms only made a light whack sound on his shirt. Her palms stung. *Damn.* She glared up at him, but he wouldn't meet her eyes. He looked at where she touched his chest. A smudge of dirt darkened the back of her hand. Duke traced her knuckles with the tips of his fingers and then cleared his throat.

"You'll get dirty and you're fragile." His hands rubbed down along her wrists. "Everything in the workroom is too heavy for you." The contact of his skin on hers made her tingle and her stomach flutter. She was angry, that's all it was.

"I'll get dirty? Heavy? What kind of argument is that?"

"This isn't an argument. The answer is no. If you want to change our routine, we probably should discuss it and look at all the alternatives from every side. Perhaps we should think it through all the way."

"Probably? Perhaps?" Tea stepped away from him and wrapped her arms around her waist. She hugged her baggy sweatshirt closer to her body. "You don't understand."

"*You* don't understand." Duke returned to where he normally worked at the table and bent his head over the large battery he'd built. Her eyes popped to the door. She should leave, walk out. The boys wouldn't even miss her.

He glanced at her only a moment before picking up a set of wire cutters. He would ignore her now just like Baron did. Every day was always the same.

"Why don't you nap?"

"You can go fuck yourself then take a nap."

Duke's head snapped up, and his eyebrows disappeared into his hair. She ignored his stunned expression.

"I just wanted to do something around here. Be useful or helpful. You and Baron are so generous, and I…" Tea bit down on her lip to keep it from trembling. She refused to cry like a child. "I wanted to be helpful for no other reason than I thought you'd appreciate it. I know I don't have my strength and I'm not valuable, but you and Baron are unfeeling bastards." There was no trade for favors, no slavery, no exchange. Why didn't they get that? "I'm more than a throw pillow." Tea spun around and stomped to the bedroom door. She threw it open and then stopped. "Damn you and your brother. I'm not a teacup."

Tea slammed the door and leaned against the wood. The tears she'd held back began to slip down her cheeks. It appeared you would contract kindness like an illness if you were around it a lot. Who knew?

Chapter 11

"What's with the box?"

Tea sat on the bed brushing her hair, listening to Duke in the other room. They hadn't talked the rest of the afternoon, and she wasn't sure what happened now. If the boys kicked her out, bring it on. She couldn't keep being nothing to them. Tea wasn't a worthless junkyard dog. Somewhere along the way she began to believe she deserved better.

"It's a box of clothes for Tea and a book."

Tea rose and tiptoed to the door. She peeked through the crack. Baron had come home early. He stood next to the couch with a cardboard box clutched in his hands.

"You got her clothes? Why?" Duke came around his work table and tossed his goggles next to the battery.

"I think she was mad at me this morning." Baron sighed.

"Join the club, dude." Duke opened the box and peeked in. "How did you get her clothes?"

"I told Doctor Mather that I wanted to dress as a woman." Baron's comment was casual, but Tea saw what was coming next.

"You did what!" Duke exploded. His flabbergasted sputtering made her smile. Why was he even surprised at his brother anymore? She certainly wasn't.

"I couldn't say *you* wanted to dress like a woman. He still thinks you're suicidal. He might start asking questions if I said it was you."

"I think he's going to ask questions no matter what." Duke exhaled as he shoved his hands into his pockets. She agreed. "I wish you would think before you speak."

"Don't worry. It's bad—" Baron closed the lid on the box and headed toward the bedroom.

"—for your health," Duke finished.

Quickly, Tea spun around and returned to the bed. She picked up her brush. She was still upset with them. Clothes weren't going to change anything. She was worth more than this.

"Tea?" Baron called as he entered the room. "What are you doing?"

When Baron spotted her, he moved just inside the room. Duke was behind him and the older twin leaned against the door frame. She turned her back on both men, so she wouldn't throw the brush at their heads. The only thing that stopped her was the fact she couldn't pick which twin to hit.

"I'm taking a nap." She glowered at the wall. "Trinkets don't do anything." Tea tossed the brush on the floor and then crossed her arms. She was acting childish, she realized that, but if they treated her like a child, then she might as well act like one.

"I'm sorry about that, Tea-cup." Baron rubbed her shoulder. She wanted to tell him to go away, but his fingers had that magical soothing quality that always got to her. *Damn.*

"Don't call her Tea-cup, dude," Duke warned.

"I came to talk to you about what I said." Baron set the box in front of her on the floor and then knelt next to her. "I know I told you to nap, but—"

"You told her to nap?" Duke sat next to her at the foot of the bed. His thigh brushed hers. "When?"

She shot him a brief look over her shoulder.

"This morning, Tea asked if she could cook, and I said no. I told her to nap." Baron leaned his head until he was in her line of sight. She glared up at the ceiling. "I didn't think that through. I'll give you that."

"Outstanding. We both did it," Duke snapped at Baron.

Tea dropped her stare to the bedspread to avoid Baron's penetrating sapphire eyes.

"What did you say?" Baron hopped to his feet coming toe-to-toe with his brother.

"I told her she couldn't help me in my storage room. No wonder she's mad at us. Great job, pig-face." Duke got up from the bed with a growl. He paced by the door. "How are you going to fix this?"

"Me? It's not all my fault she's mad. You told her 'no' too. This time you didn't think it through." Baron faced Duke blocking Duke's restless stomping back and forth. "What happened to looking at things from all angles?" Baron punched him in the shoulder. Duke shoved him back, but Baron remained solid.

"You've no idea how to talk to a woman," Duke snapped. "Especially a beautiful and complicated woman like our Tea. You messed this up."

"And you know what to say to women?" Another shove.

"More than you do." Another punch. "Pinhead." Duke's eye started to swell shut. The older twin nailed Baron in the jaw in return.

"Low blow." Baron wiped the blood from his lip. "I'm not dumb."

"This is your fault." Duke raised his fist. "You shouldn't have—"

"Timeout," she called when Duke grabbed the front of Baron's shirt. "If you want to talk to a woman, you have one. I'm right here."

They may say they didn't need her to do anything but drink water and nap, but that wasn't true. The twins needed a girlfriend.

Both men hurried to her side.

"We want to talk to you and—" Duke sat down next to her again. He rubbed her shoulders.

"—we don't want to fight." Baron came around and knelt at her feet.

"Sorry, little Tea." Duke sighed. "If you want to cook, that's fine."

"As long as you *choose* to do it." Baron pulled a cookbook out of the box. He held the red-and-white binder toward her. "After you said you were a slave with your grandma, I thought cooking might make you feel like a servant."

"We don't want you here as a servant or a slave. It's why I don't like it when you do the laundry." Duke added.

"I don't like it when you clean the kitchen or fix the furniture." Baron stared at the binder in his hands.

"You never have to do anything to be with us."

"I like to fix the furniture or pick up. I do those things because I want to. Not because you're making me." The twins never forced her to do anything. She was free here. "I want to cook. I thought it'd be fun." Tea hesitated, then she took the binder from his outstretched hands. "I hate the applesauce." She traced the faded words "Bet Home and Gard" on the front.

"I know the applesauce isn't the best." Baron ran a finger along the edge of the book.

"The applesauce tastes like chunky earwax paste, dude." Duke got off the bed. "You don't have to repay us for staying here, Tea. After you told me about your life, I didn't want you to think you had to work here either. At night when you talk, it scares me that you don't think of yourself as anything other than an animal. You're so much more than that, and I don't know how to say it. I thought you'd get tired and dirty in the stockroom." Duke shoved his hands in his pockets. "I don't want you to be bored." His eyes captured hers. "If you want to organize tools in the storeroom, that's fine as long as—"

"—you don't lift anything heavy," Baron finished.

Tea smiled. Someone telling her not to lift anything heavy was comical.

Duke pulled his hands from his pockets and knelt next to his brother. "This is your home, Tea."

"We want you content, Tea-cup."

She went to open her mouth, but Baron took her by the hand before she said a word, "I don't think of you like an item or a trinket. I know you're a person. It's just an endearment that bugs Duke."

"I think the only hobby you have is bugging each other." Tea hugged the book to her chest.

"Ha." Baron laughed. "Fighting with each other and yoga."

"We don't know how to talk to women." Duke sighed. "I'm trying, Tea."

"I don't mind the nickname, Baron." Tea lifted her eyes to look at both men. "There isn't a special way either of you have to talk to me. I only wanted…" She paused. "I want to be here in your home as more than a throw pillow."

"I don't want you so bored that you'd kill yourself." Baron gave Duke a pointed look.

"He didn't say he was bored. He said he was lonely." Tea smiled at the box he carried in with the cookbook.

"Nothing wrong with your memory." Duke pushed the box closer to her.

She'd never had a home before or people who cared about her wellbeing. She didn't know what to do or say.

"Thank you." The words sounded fake, but she meant them. The only safe place to look was the carpet.

"We want you to be happy." Duke grabbed her chin and tipped her so she gazed at him.

"What does that mean?"

"Why do you always ask us that?" Duke let go of her. "It means we want our friend to be happy. There's no hidden agenda."

"We're friends?" Tea's eyes widened. "I've never had one of those, let alone two of them."

"Aren't we?" Baron asked. "I know I haven't been around since the hospital is slammed, but I thought we were friends." He glanced at Duke as if searching his face for confirmation. "I thought you said things were fine. You talk to her at night."

"I thought things were fine." Duke scanned her. "And I know I've been busy too, but I told you I'm behind on my work." Duke glanced at his brother, then back at her. "You talk to Baron over dinner and late into the evening. You sit with him when he shaves. I thought that meant you liked him."

"I like you both."

"Okay, then. Once we both catch up, we'll all settle into a comfortable routine, won't we?" Duke's eyes searched hers expectantly. "We'll say the right things, Tea."

"Things will settle. And for now, whatever you want, say the word."

"Everything is fine." Tea hugged the cookbook.

The twins did that smirk like they didn't believe her. Baron tipped his head to the side as Duke stood and raised one eyebrow.

"Honestly, I'm content here. You don't have to talk to me in any special way." As she spoke, Tea realized her life was better here than anywhere else she'd ever been. That was scarier than facing a train-full of furious harvesters. Tea didn't want them to wake up one day and want her gone. "It was only that I've never sat around like this before. I've worked my whole life." She bit her bottom lip. "I want to be valuable, like when I had my gift. My life might've been crummy, but I was prized, and there was always something to do."

"You're valuable to us." Duke's hand stroked her shoulder. "No gift necessary. We don't want to treat you like a prize or a trophy."

"You can stay here no matter what you do." Baron pushed his box closer to her. "We can keep you entertained."

"Entertained?" Tea grinned. Now would be the time to tell them that it would entertain her if she could kiss them. If she could do that, she wouldn't need the cookbook.

The knock on the front door was more of a loud banging than a regular thump. Duke and Baron jumped to their feet. Tea tensed. Her plan to talk to the twins about kissing was put on hold.

For one second, she'd gotten used to not being consumed or beaten down. After only a short time of being in their home, she hated the idea of being ripped from her haven. Somewhere along the way, the twins' apartment had become her sanctuary.

"Stay here," Baron said to her as he rushed out of the bedroom. Duke was hot on his brother's heels.

After they left the room, Tea hurried to the door and peeked through the crack. Her heart pounded. She expected the H.S.P.C. Just when things would've gotten better with the twins, agents would show up and take her away. The idea of losing the boys disturbed her to her very core. For all her complaints about being nothing more than a trinket, her life was better here than anywhere else she'd ever been. No one hurt her. She was free to speak without getting slapped.

"Who are you?" Tea could hear Duke's voice rough and deep. Tea spotted the older twin filling up the doorway, but she couldn't see if it was agents in the hall.

Whoever was on the other side of the door might challenge her new fragile world. Once again, she wished she had her gift. *Damn*, she wished again. If she had her strength, she could fight to stay with Baron and Duke. She would protect them.

Tea gasped when she realized she would kill for them. She would do anything they asked, and her devotion had nothing to do with force or servitude. She liked them. Really liked them. When the hell had that happened?

"I want the remains of Teagan. Where's the body?"

Chapter 12

Tea knew the voice. Fear froze her to the spot. The Originals had come for her.

As she pressed her face closer to the door frame, a shiver shot down her spine. Silo Fletcher stood in the doorway to the twins' apartment. Silo was a replica of his father, Fletcher Davis. The Original member had put on a little more weight, but the black eyes, hair, and skin looked exactly the same.

Tea held her breath as Silo shoved Duke. The older twin rocked back on his heels, and The Original member entered their home. Tea's heart continued its furious pounding as she watched Silo's commanding figure.

"Who are you?" Baron asked as he entered.

Silo was alone. That was a plus, but she still shook.

Baron planted himself in front of Silo when he stepped around the broken battery.

"Get out of my way." With flowing grace, Silo crossed the room in swift strides to the kitchen. He went directly to the small closet that held the brooms. He looked inside and then slammed the door shut. Next, he strode around the kitchen island.

"There's no dead body here," Baron pointed to the exit.

Tea let go of the door and stepped backward expecting Silo to throw open the bedroom door next.

"Get out," she heard Duke command.

Tea peeked through the crack in the door again.

Duke stood in Silo's path. Silo shoved the twin. Duke caught Silo's wrists and flung them back.

"I don't think you know who you're dealing with," Silo spat. "But you will."

Baron stepped up next to his brother. "We don't care who you are. Get out."

Tea held her breath. Maybe the twins would be scary enough that Silo would give up. She'd seen them scrap. They could pummel Silo, except she knew The Original member's gift.

Tea bit her bottom lip hard enough that she tasted blood.

Silo stepped backward as he took a canteen from his belt. Tea tensed. She would have to speak up even if she wanted to hide. He unscrewed the cap with a flick of his thumb. She would have to call out, even if that meant going back to a gang of cutthroats. Tea dug deep for the courage to face her past.

She gripped the door handle. To protect her twins, Tea would have to do the right thing. She was about as good at doing the right thing as she was at offering comfort.

The canteen was open. The cap spun on the floor. Silo's fingers gracefully twirled in the air. Water floated out of the container with a whoosh. Silo's gift of being able to command liquid, and his signature move of drowning people, would destroy her twins. As she stepped out of the room, the murky brown water rushed at Duke and Baron. She had to help.

Damn. Too late.

"Silo." Tea didn't let her fear show. The Originals could smell fear.

"That didn't take long." Silo smiled.

The water went into both men's mouth and nose. The twins tried to gulp for air, but there was none. Duke threw his hands out like the action might stop the liquid. His arms swinging did nothing. She knew that. Tea knew what Silo could do.

"If you drown my match, I'll kill you and all your sons." She might not have her strength, but what she said was true. Tea would kill him and every kid he'd created. And Silo had made quite a few little ones.

Duke and Baron dropped to the floor. Baron's hands scratched at his throat. Suddenly, they both heaved. Their backs arched. Their bodies were completely dry, but they coughed and spurted water as if they'd drowned in a pool. As they struggled to suck air into their lungs, both of their faces turned a red-blue as they hacked and vomited.

Silo paid them no attention.

Tea walked around the couch to keep space between her and Silo. As she moved, she realized she might have to go back to The Originals. Mother or no Mother, she didn't want to go back, especially with no gift to protect her. The Originals would eat her alive. She wanted to be left alone.

Tea's eyes jumped to the twins puking dirty water onto the floor. Okay, so not left *alone*, left with these two men.

"Conpar?" Silo shifted closer to her. She kept walking so the furniture was always between them.

"Yes."

Conpar was Mother's word for match. A pair was the only thing respected by The Originals. She tipped her chin up and gave nothing away. The twins weren't her match as far as she could tell, but she wouldn't let on.

"I came to get your body. Once I have you, I can finally call for a new leader. Mother and Weaver are dead. The H.S.P.C. gave them Snow Flu for study. I have Mother's ashes. I got Weaver's braid." Silo held up a black braid and then shoved the hair back into his pocket.

"I'm not going back." Tea scooted around the kitchen counter. "Not me, not my body, nothing."

Silo glanced at Duke and Baron struggling to catch their breath. They spat as they got to their knees. Silo held up one hand and began to twirl his fingers in a circle. As his hand made a wide loop, the water collected off the floor. The dark stream floated in front of the twin's faces. Both the twins eyed the hovering puddle wearily. No one moved.

"You'd be the leader if you returned alive." Silo shaped the water into a dagger with a wave.

Tea had thought of that. If she went with Silo, she could have The Originals at her feet. They would let her take charge. That is until they found out she didn't have her strength. Who knows what would happen after her secret was discovered? Then once they knew about the baby, all hell would break loose. She carried an H.S.P.C. baby. They might kill her because of the child alone.

"Without me, you'll be the leader," Tea pointed out. No, she wasn't going with him. Tea was sure that's what Silo wanted anyway. "Take the spot, Silo. You're powerful enough. They'll follow you. You're Fletcher's bloodline."

"And what if you change your mind?" Silo stirred the water in the air. The liquid looked like a mini floating whirlpool as it followed his movements.

"I'm not going back. I'm dead. Do you understand me, Silo?" Tea walked to Duke's work table. She picked up a tin and poured out the wire nuts. Once the container was empty, she swiped all the metal shavings and dust and dirt from the table. When the tin was full of the charred ash, she snapped on the lid and then faced Silo again. "Here are my ashes. Take this. If I have anyone else show up on my doorstep, they'll be dead before they cross the threshold. And my reach includes my twins." She inclined her head toward Duke and Baron. They both still labored for air. "If they come for me, I'll come for you."

Silo studied her face. "You've backed me up a time or two. I don't want to fight you."

"I've backed you up more times than that." Tea glared.

"You're dead." Silo lifted his hand. Tea felt her shirt cling to her back. Her eyes focused on his fingers. The slightest twitch and she would have to act fast.

Silo took the tin.

Tea held in her relief.

Silo turned around and headed for the door. She kept her face neutral, ignoring the urge to check on the twins.

The Original member held the doorknob and turned to her. "I won't be seeing you again, Teagan."

She didn't nod. She didn't speak. Tea didn't move. He left and shut the door quietly behind him. The water splashed to the tiles.

Tea hurried over to Duke and Baron. She dropped to her knees next to them and rubbed Duke's back.

"I think I might throw up." Duke gagged. "That water was probably not clean."

"I know it wasn't." Baron coughed, and she patted him on the back. "I think we should go to the hospital." He wheezed. "But—"

"—we don't want to leave you alone," Duke finished the sentence and then spurted up water again.

Tea helped Baron to his feet. In turn, Baron reached for his brother. Duke spit and saliva dribbled down his chin.

"I'll be fine. Go. Don't worry. It's bad for your health."

Duke snickered and then coughed. "Nothing wrong with your memory."

"Lock the door, Tea-cup." Baron pointed to the door as he held his brother.

"I will."

Chapter 13

Tea soaked in a hot bath while she waited for the twins. She'd had to do something to get her mind off how they could've died. Mother did terrible things over the years, but for the first time, she felt a deep emotion about the violence she'd witnessed. If she kept thinking about what had happened, she would go insane. She'd taken a bath as a last-ditch effort to stop herself from running to the hospital.

Right as she wrapped a towel around her body, she heard them enter the front door. Tea hurried out of the bathroom and met them as they reached the sofa.

"Did you miss us?" Duke came to an abrupt halt. Baron smiled at her as he threw his coat on the rack near the bedroom door.

"No, I…" she started to lie then changed her mind. They were supposed to be her friends, and she was working on being a decent, honest person. Well, maybe not *totally* honest. She was hiding from the H.S.P.C. "Yes. I was scared for you both. Are you alright?"

"Fine." Baron nodded. "But we owe you a thank-you, Tea. You—"

"—saved our lives." Duke came around the couch and pulled her into a brief hug before leaning back.

Tea wrapped her arms around her middle. She didn't know how to accept a thank-you. She'd never received one before.

"I didn't do anything."

Baron pulled her into a quick hug. "You could've stayed hidden or—"

"—you could've let him kill us then gone back to The Originals." Duke ran his hand down her arm. "He said you'd be the leader."

Tea pulled away from them. The praise made her uncomfortable. "I should've come out sooner. If I'd made a faster decision, you wouldn't have gotten hurt at all."

"You don't know if that's true or not." Baron patted her arm. "Besides, you didn't sit around and ponder it as long as Duke would have."

"Low blow, Baron," Tea pointed out.

"Baron's right." Duke shoved his hands into his pockets. "You don't know what would've happened, and I'm grateful for everything you did."

"Silo could've killed you. He wouldn't have given it a second thought." Tea shuddered to think about what could've happened. "Yes. I thought about going back, and I shouldn't have even considered it. I won't choose that life for the baby or me. Besides, without my gift, I'd be a sitting elk."

"They don't know you lost your gift." Duke walked to the counter. "That guy Silo was afraid of you."

"I used to be strong." Tea followed Duke to the kitchen. "In the past, I could've crushed him. I actually didn't know what to do when he showed up. The only thing I could think of was saying you were both my match. I'm happy he bought it."

"Why did you say that?" Baron studied her.

"A true match is one of the few things respected by The Originals. Our leader, Mother, she called it 'Conpar' which is Latin for…" Tea tried to remember Mother's rant. There were too many. "I think it means pair or mate. She honored a match. She always worked to find me one. Mother wanted pairs that were the same nationality or bloodline. Pureblood. I met a lot of Cuban's, both men and women, but none matched with me. Mother was forever trying to make the perfect people who would take over the planet. Mother believed that the best-gifted people would be the ones of a pure race."

"We aren't Cuban." Duke raised an eyebrow. "I could point out our hair and skin—"

"—for a start." Baron smiled.

"I know." Tea grinned. "I've never told anyone this, but I'm not a full Cuban either. My dad was Cuban, but not my mom. I don't know what I am exactly. A mix of things, I guess. I never asked."

"If you're not Cuban, why did Mother think you were?" Baron asked.

"Mother kept a boy who claimed he could tell peoples ancestry. Everyone knew he was faking it, but we didn't want Mother to kill him for lying. He said I was full-blooded Cuban, so I went with it. I picked up some Spanish, rolled my 'r's, and pretended. I didn't have to try too hard. Mother wanted my gift. That's all she ever cared about."

"If The Originals believe in pairs of the same race, why did Silo accept that we are a match?" Duke pulled dried meat out of the fridge and tossed the package onto the counter. "You know there are two of us."

"She can count," Baron scoffed.

"Silo and some of the others don't care about race or number or anything like that. They think it's about chemistry and having a feeling or simply knowing when you've connected. He respected that I said you were mine. It's all that matters. I won't be seeing him again." Tea hoped that was true. Either that, or if they did see him again, she would have her gift back by then.

"I'm surprised he didn't question that we weren't one person for you. We're twins." The words had just left Baron's mouth when there was another loud bang on the door.

"You're getting the door this time." Duke glared at Baron. "I did it last time."

"No."

"Yes."

"No."

The knocking came again as Baron punched Duke in the stomach.

"Timeout." Tea held up her hand. "Baron, get the door. I doubt it's Silo again."

"Hide, Tea." Baron waved at Duke. "Hurry in case—"

"—Silo has come back to drown us again?" Duke grabbed Tea's hand.

"I won't let you drown." Tea was propelled toward the broom closet and shoved inside. "You said you would never shove me into a closet."

"I'm sorry, Tea." Duke's shoulders dropped. "I told you I'm not good at talking to women. Apparently, never say never."

"If it's Silo, I can talk to him." The door closed on her words.

"Stay in there until we know who it is," Duke whispered. "I'll be a second."

Again, Tea found herself squinting to see through the crack of the door. Listening at doors was becoming a popular pastime for her.

Baron swung the front door open with the stiffness of a sentry.

"Doctor Mather?" Baron announced as his shoulders sagged. "What are you doing here?"

Tea couldn't hear the doctor's response, but Baron spoke after a quick glance at Duke. "No, Duke's not around, and I was about to get some rest. Can I talk to you later?"

Tea heard muffled speech, and then Baron used the hand behind the door to wave at Duke.

"No, no." Baron wildly gestured at Duke. "I guess if you want to come in for a minute, it's fine."

Duke ran around the kitchen island, and to her shock, he climbed into the closet with her. He pushed her shoulder and squeezed past the mop and broom. Tea was plastered against a drying rack as she worked to squish herself backward as far as she could go. In the end, she ended up face-to-chest with Duke.

"What're you doing?" she hissed as she leaned around him to look out the crack in the door.

"Baron said I'm not home. I had to go somewhere. I couldn't make it to the bedroom or my workroom without being seen. This won't be long. Shush." He put his hand over her mouth. Tea yanked down his hand and then found a spot where she could see Doctor Mather entering the apartment.

Tea had heard about Baron's doctor friend on many occasions. He was the only person at the hospital who liked the younger twin.

As the doctor marched into the apartment, Tea thought he was more handsome than she had pictured. Doctor

Mather was shorter than her twins, but she figured most men were. The doctor had a deep tan, as if he spent time with a set of sunlamps, and thick black hair. He wore light-green scrubs as if he'd just come from the hospital. The doctor strode in and halted next to the counter. He didn't look happy and tapped his pristine tennis shoes as he crossed his arms over his chest. His plump lips flattened into a grim line.

"What's going on with you, Baron?" Mather combed his fingers through his short black hair and then rubbed the back of his neck as he scanned the room. "I'm asking as your friend. Not as your doctor and not as a boss. Duke isn't around, so I'd like you to speak candidly."

"Nothing." Baron's eyes went to the cupboard and then returned to his friend. "I'm going to get some sleep. I'll see you tomorrow."

Mather threw up his hands.

"That's the wrong answer," Duke whispered in her ear.

"Geeze, nothing is wrong? Do you know what this is?" Mather pulled out a needle and slapped the syringe down on the counter. "This is the best immobilization drug we have. I brought it here because I thought I might have to subdue you."

"What?" Baron picked up the needle and toyed with it in his hands. "This is for crazy people we have to restrain at the hospital. It knocks them out."

"I've been given that before," she whispered to Duke. "Doesn't last long."

"Yes. I know what it's for." Mather walked back and forth. "Tell me if this doesn't sound like a crazy person. First, you tell me Duke took a bunch of drugs. Most of them I don't even know where he got them. And you just give me a casual phone call where you insisted that you don't want to bring him into the hospital." Mather turned and paced in front of the kitchen counter. "Then when I see you again, you tell me you want to wear women's clothing and that you want to start reading cookbooks in your spare time."

"I—" Baron began, but the doctor threw up both his hands again.

"I'm not done," he snapped. "And now today, when I get to work, they tell me that you and Duke took a bath together, and you both slipped at the same time and then fell and almost drowned." Mather stopped and gave a pointed look.

"I don't envy Baron," Duke whispered. Tea bit her lip. She had no idea how Baron was going to explain all this away.

"I'm going through a phase," Baron said weakly as his eyes went to the closet. Nervous that they might see her, Tea shifted and stared at Duke's chest.

"A phase that involves taking a bath with your twin? You're not a two-year-old, Baron!"

Tea involuntarily recoiled. As soon as she moved, her shoulder bumped the broom to her right. Duke caught the top. She grasped the handle in the middle. She went perfectly still. That was close.

Duke glared down at her.

She mouthed the words "I got it."

"Is this an incest thing? I know people say that about you and Duke, but I've always thought it was a rumor." Mather paused. "Are you having sex with your brother?"

"That's what people say about you?" Tea tilted her head to capture Duke's eyes in the darkness. He looked away.

"No. I'm not…" Baron faltered. "It's not incest." Baron's words sounded miserable.

Mather's voice grabbed her attention again. "Did you talk to Duke about his suicide attempt?"

Tea wanted to look through the crack to see Baron's face. She pressed forward and brushed against Duke. His hard body tugged at her chest like her heart beat toward him. The feel of his frame so close caught her off guard. She forgot she was wearing only a towel. Tea leaned back from the warmth beckoning her toward the older twin. Her hip caught the dustpan.

Again, she reached out before the tool would have fallen to the floor.

"Stop moving." Duke took the broom out of her hand. As soon as he grabbed the bristles, the handle bumped a feather duster behind his head. Tea reached behind him and caught the item, but now she was plastered against his chest. She couldn't see in the dark to hang up the damn pan. She froze and peeked out the door. Doctor Mather hopped around and still blustered. He didn't hear them, thank God.

Duke wrapped an arm around her waist as she halted. The weight of his hands tugged on her towel. The cloth slipped, but to save her modesty, she would have to drop the dustpan or the feather duster. She bid the fabric goodbye.

Duke didn't seem to pay any attention to her predicament or his brother's conversation. His hand was on one end of the broom, but the other slipped up her back. When he found her skin, his fingers spread wide. He pushed, and the towel fell. It made a quiet thump.

Duke's mouth descended. Tea was completely absorbed by the feel of him as her naked body pressed against his clothing. Duke didn't kiss anything like Baron. There was a gentleness, a sipping on her lips, followed by a leisurely licking of her mouth as he took his time. Duke kissed like he was learning her mouth. There was only need and warmth. Fire blossomed in her chest. The heat was unlike anything she'd ever felt before. He continued the sweet assault. She only barely kept herself from moaning. His mouth on hers was too incredible. Too amazing.

She wanted the twins. Was this what a true match felt like when they connected?

The door to the closet was yanked open. Tea dropped the items in her hands and scooped up her towel. Baron glared at his brother; then his eyes scanned her as she clutched the towel to her naked body. His cheeks flushed. The younger twin looked furious and flustered.

Tea stepped out of the closet past an irate Baron. Duke dropped the broom.

"What the fuck do you think you were doing? I was talking to Doctor Mather," Baron shouted at his brother. "Now he thinks I like him."

"You did it to me," Duke flung back. "I burned myself."

"I didn't know what you were doing." Baron fumed. "You knew I was talking to my boss. Now he thinks I've lost my mind."

"You have lost your mind."

"So have you."

Both men looked at her. Again, she supposed she should help, maybe call a timeout. She opened her mouth then closed her lips. She didn't know what this was about exactly.

"Tea," Duke took a deep breath, "Baron and I need to discuss a few things."

Discuss meant punch.

Baron gave her a warm smile. "Why don't you finish your bath and put on warm clothes. Take a—"

"Don't say nap," Duke said quickly.

"You could read your cookbook." Baron gestured to the bedroom door. "If you want anything, say the word."

Tea turned around and headed toward the bedroom. A part of her thought to stay and eavesdrop, but she'd had enough of listening at doors for one day. She trembled from that kiss, and she needed to take a second to get her head together. She needed some time to figure out what game she was playing.

Right as she swung the door closed, Duke threw the first punch.

Chapter 14

Before the day began, Tea got Baron ice for his black eye or his bruised knuckles while he got ready for work. After he headed to the hospital, she made Duke breakfast while he was in the shower. Even when she burned the eggs or added too much salt, the older twin never complained.

Duke would simply sit across from her holding ice to whatever part of him was injured in the previous fight. As he shoveled food into his mouth, he told her what projects he had to accomplish. After breakfast, he did the dishes while she gathered the items Duke needed from the storeroom.

Life with her twins was good.

The next few days flew. The twins made Tea happier than she'd ever been. The only blemish on her otherwise perfect world was her perpetual attraction to Duke and Baron which didn't dissipate and seemed to fuel the boxing matches.

Tea flopped down on her belly on Duke's bed. She glanced at the time. It was 2:30 in the afternoon. Her new habit was to start cooking dinner early, so the meal would be ready when Baron came home from the hospital.

To help manage the ever-growing disquiet, Tea cooked as she convinced herself that her lust was all in her head. The lie never worked. She wanted them. Both. If Tea wanted to stay in the sunny world she now lived in, a choice had to be made. Tea had seen them fight. She refused to end up as an object fought over.

Tea flipped open another cookbook Baron had given her yesterday. As she wrote a list of ingredients, she adjusted the straps on her dress. Cooking had become her only outlet for the stress. The hobby curbed her desire for the twins. Cooking didn't always work, but the activity lessened the longing.

After she'd kissed Duke during Mather's visit, Duke seemed to decide never to talk about it. He also never let that kind of intimacy happen again. Baron never mentioned his kiss with her either. The younger twin still kissed her on the tip of her nose, but both men were distant. They didn't even hug her anymore. There was now a clear boundary. Duke stopped cuddling with her at night. The more space there was between them, the more her desire for them multiplied. Wanting her cake and eating it too left her with neither. Loneliness chipped away at her bliss.

The boys handled the chasm by thrashing each other every chance they got.

Baron's voice floated in from the living room. Tea lifted her head from her book. He must be home early again. Doctor Mather had given him extra time off ever since he lied about taking a bath with Duke. In a few dinner conversations, she gathered that Mather thought Baron was overworked. Mather believed Baron's anomalous behavior would mellow if he had more time to himself. As far as Tea was concerned, she thought the extra time at home made the fighting worse, but she couldn't say that. If she brought up the violence, she was afraid of what might happen.

Tea sat up as Baron entered the bedroom, pulling off his shirt.

"Stop asking. I'm so sick of this." Duke followed him.

"What if we do yoga and—" Baron's eyes raked her body. His words dangled in the air unfinished. Duke didn't finish his brother's sentence for the first time since she met them.

His eyes went wide. Today she was doing what she always did. Tea was on one of their beds, reading and picking what she wanted to prepare for dinner. Most of the time she gave the twins a list of supplies from her book.

Both men stared as she rose with her paper clutched in her hand. The look on their faces appeared to be shock and... horror.

"What's wrong?" She held out her list. Baron took the paper automatically and then shoved the list at Duke's chest. Duke's eyes went from the top of her head to her toes as he grasped the scrap.

"That dress was in the box I gave you?" Baron looked around for the cardboard carton, but yesterday Tea had hung all the clothes in the closet.

Tea glanced down at her dress. She'd made the garment a few days ago, but this afternoon was the first time she'd worn the outfit. Her garb wasn't a dress exactly. The clothing was three wide colorful scarves she'd woven and tied together.

"What happened to the big robe or—"

"—my sweatpants and shirt?" Duke asked. "You weren't wearing *that* this morning." Duke pointed at her accusingly and then turned to Baron. "This is your fault. You should've talked to me first. You didn't think this through."

Tea thought she looked fine. In fact, she thought she looked pretty. The yellows and greens made her darker skin tone glow.

"She needs a hoodie." Baron grabbed one out of the dresser. He held the top out. "You'll get cold." Before she could protest, he pulled the oversized sweatshirt over her head.

"I'm not cold." Tea pushed the hood out of her face and then shoved her arms through the sleeves.

Duke and Baron passed a private conversation between them. They then looked back at her.

"I'll get these food items for you." Baron grabbed at the paper, and with his other hand, he pushed her out the door of the bedroom.

"Put these on too." Duke took sweatpants out of the closet and shoved them into her arms. "Perhaps more layers would help."

Confused, Tea took the huge gray sweatpants as she was thrust into the living room.

"We're going to do yoga, and then we'll have dinner with you. Duke and I have to talk." Baron shut the door behind her.

"Talk" usually meant fight. So did "discuss," "chat," and "have a meeting." Tea paused next to the sofa and stared at the sweatpants in her arms. *Damn.* What happened?

Tea adjusted the pants in her arms and slipped off the sweater. As she folded the garments, she glanced down at her dress. She thought she looked cute. She'd brushed her hair until the curls had a shine. This was the first time in her whole life she felt beautiful and content. A pang twisted inside of her. She was… hurt. She'd never felt this kind of disappointment before.

Tea had been put down and insulted more times than she could count, but never had someone's words mattered. She had always endured. But this time, she'd been wounded without being called even one nasty name.

Shaking her head, Tea smiled to herself. *Damn.* They probably sincerely thought she was cold. Baron was always concerned about her health. She would tell them she was fine and then see if she could hang out in the bedroom and watch them exercise.

Seeing the twins bend over was her favorite. Most of the time they didn't wear shirts. She couldn't have them, but that didn't stop her from enjoying the way their bodies flowed from one position to another. Before she met them, she didn't even know what yoga was. Now yoga was her favorite part of the day.

Spinning around, she walked back over to the bedroom. Opening the door slightly, the first words she heard stopped her from entering.

"Are you going to tell her that she isn't pregnant?" Duke asked.

"It would be the right thing to do but—"

"—if we tell her, she'll leave." Duke turned his head. They appeared to share another one of those silent conversations. Those were getting on her nerves.

Both men bent forward and faced the opposite wall. The beds had been pushed to the far corner and their backs were to the door. They didn't see her head poking past the doorjamb. Tea opened her mouth, then closed it again.

"Tea could go—"

"—and if she left then perhaps…"

Tea hung on the word *perhaps*.

"Don't say probably or perhaps to me, bro. Right now, I don't know how to live with Tea. I'm so sick of this."

"Don't think that it's any easier for me," Duke snapped. "Don't act like I'm happy about this."

Tea hugged the clothing to her chest. Thinking they didn't like her dress hurt, but hearing their unhappiness was a searing pain that scorched her heart. Tea angrily swiped at the tears that gathered. She turned away, but Baron's next sentence caught her attention again.

"How about a prostitute? I hear Rena is back. She's willing." Baron shifted forward. Both men went down into a slow push-up. On a normal day, the muscles in their arms would have all her attention. Right now, their lick-able skin wasn't distracting her. Her ears were on fire. They wanted a hooker but not her.

"She'd probably deal with us, but she doesn't like us."

"That's nothing new," Baron scoffed.

Cold fury shimmered in her belly. The twins were hers. No one could have them.

Duke and Baron bent over, favoring her with the sight of their perfectly rounded asses again. Those butts were hers. She opened her mouth, but Duke spoke before she had a chance.

"We're low on HOCs. We got probably enough money for a hand job. Is that even worth it?"

Tea's eyes widened. Her body trembled with the need to either tell them off or scream. The worst thing—they didn't even ask her. She would jerk them off. Tea would do more than that. Ideas of all the ways she could touch the twins shimmered in her brain. The sexual positions brought a smile to her face. She did want to be helpful. They should ask her.

"It's better that than what we're doing now," Baron growled. "Thanks for that by the way."

Both men came to a standing pose with their arms above their heads.

Tea leaned back slowly and closed the door. She didn't pull the knob all the way tight in case the latch would make a click. Getting caught eavesdropping wouldn't be helpful in this situation. If she got caught watching them do yoga, she wouldn't care. Often, she waltzed into the room and sat on the bed while she pretended to read. Tea liked seeing all their gorgeous muscles bend and flex, but this time she absolutely didn't want to get discovered.

This time they would know she heard them making plans.

Tea glared at the closed door. She should tell them the truth. She should ask them. That's what a decent person would do. Tea should say what's on her mind... except, in the past, that never went well.

Leaning against the wall next to the door, Tea wrapped her head around the three things she'd learned. She wasn't pregnant. On some level, she had that feeling already. It bothered her that they didn't tell her right away. That led her to the next problem... It sounded like they wanted her to leave. If she had done something they didn't like, they should explain. She could fix the issue. Mother was never shy about telling her to do all sorts of things.

Tea squeezed Duke's massive gray sweatshirt. Quickly, she pulled the top over her head.

If they didn't like her dress, fine. She slipped the knot loose. The dress dropped to the floor. She pulled on the loose sweatpants. Picking up the dress, she held the lovely fabric out and stared at the bright colors.

It wasn't about the dress. It was about her. Why wasn't she good enough? Why was a prostitute better? She could do whatever Rena did. Tea could probably do it better. She wasn't a fragile porcelain teacup. Her grandmother and Mother had beaten that right out of her. Tea was tough, and the idea of two men didn't scare her. If it were two strangers, she might be frightened, but they were her twins. They belonged with her. She'd been with them for weeks.

Her past nagged that she should keep her mouth shut. Her fingers traced the scar around her neck.

Fear that they would toss her out for opening her mouth tormented her. In one moment, all her joy was swept away by one word that kept spinning around in her head.

Rena.

Chapter 15

Dinner was tense. Breakfast the next morning wasn't better. If the twins noticed the strained silence, they didn't mention the lack of conversation. Baron only asked about her hydration and ran a thermometer across her forehead before he went to work.

During the afternoon, Tea spied Duke adjusting the temperature in the apartment. It didn't matter what the degrees were. She was covered from head to foot in the required garb that the boys wanted her to wear.

By the time Baron came home from work, Tea didn't have her feelings anymore sorted out then when she first listened in on their conversation. She cooked, but they didn't chat like normal. Perhaps she talked too much. Perhaps the twins liked the quiet, and they had never mentioned the preference before.

Damn, now she was using way too many *perhaps*.

After Baron showered and cleaned up after working at the hospital, he sat at the kitchen counter with ice on his knee. Duke joined him. Tea put away the pots and pans from the dinner she'd prepared and didn't come around to sit between them. She leaned against the stove and concentrated on her plate instead of the two men she refused to engage.

The twins rambled about the hospital, Mather, and the batteries, but she noted the looks they tossed her way. The looks were covert, but she didn't miss them.

After they ate and disappeared into the bedroom, she sat on the couch and went back and forth on her anger. She was upset, except she didn't have the right to be indignant. Duke and Baron were not her boyfriends. She didn't get to have a say on their sex life. Tea understood that, but she didn't feel that way. The one thing she should be cross about was the fact that the twins never told her she wasn't pregnant. If they wanted her to leave, why didn't they just tell her she wasn't carrying a baby? It dawned on her to ask them about that, but fear kept her tongue still. She didn't know what she would say if they told her she wasn't having a baby; therefore, she should leave. The idea made her heart lurch out of her chest. Escape had been the only thing on her mind when she showed up, but now, leaving would rip her apart.

"I forgot to give this needle back to Doctor Mather. I'll have to remember tomorrow," Baron muttered as he came out of the bedroom. He dug into the pocket of his white jacket and then tossed the garment on the coat rack by the bedroom door.

Their skin glistened with sweat, and they looked sexy. Tea's eyes always followed them after they finished their exercise. Duke returned to his battery and lifted his shirt to wipe moisture off his forehead. His abs made her mouth go dry, but in the back of her head was the thought that another woman would lick those muscles. Not her. Never her.

Duke glanced over at his brother when Baron yanked a handful of papers, three pens, and a small white envelope from his coat.

"Do you want me to get you more cookbooks, Tea-cup?" Baron crossed over to the couch. He set a letter on the table next to Duke as he passed.

When he set the paper down, Tea noted the name written neatly on the front. The word might as well have been in neon.

Rena.

Her eyes stayed glued to the note. Here it was. They would meet up with another woman. A woman who was better than Tea. A pro that they wanted. Her hands curled into fists. If her gift had returned, she would be flipping a table right about now.

"Tea?" Baron set his pens and papers on the counter. His voice cut through her thoughts.

"What?"

She stood as her hand itched to snatch that letter and crumple the paper. She didn't even care what the message said. The urge to shred it into tiny little pieces almost overwhelmed her. She forced her feet to stay rooted to the spot. If she said something, she could be out on her ass.

"Do you want a book, or should I get you more to eat? You look pale, you should—"

"Don't say nap." Duke snickered from where he swept his workspace. He stopped and scanned her. "Tea? Is something wrong?"

"Not nap." Baron smiled. "How about a drink of water?"

"I'm fine," she said through clenched teeth, but she wasn't, and they all knew it.

Tea looked everywhere in the apartment other than the paper next to Duke. She failed. Her eyes zeroed in on the letter. Duke's and Baron's gaze dropped to the letter as well.

Duke picked up the message and shoved the paper into his pocket. The corner stuck out the top.

"Tea?" Duke set the broom aside and walked toward her. "Perhaps we should work in the storeroom? I've a few things we could probably do." Duke reached for her hand, but she took a hasty step back. Touching him felt wrong. Soon his hand would wrap around another woman. His fingers could be fondling Rena's hair while that bitch stroked him to completion. Tea had seen the way his strong hands worked the wires. She would never feel that.

Closing her eyes, Tea could remember with vivid clarity Duke's palm spread across her back when they hid in the closet. She could recall the smell of the metal on his skin. She could feel the calluses. *Damn, nothing wrong with her memory.*

"Tea?" Baron asked. "What is it?"

Tea's eyes popped open. She met Baron's honest look of concern. She recalled his mouth, so hot, so hungry for her. His lips might be on Rena's, but she was the one he wanted. Tea was sure of it. She'd never been kissed the way the twins kissed her. She swallowed. There was chemistry between them. She couldn't forget.

Tea couldn't let this go. The twins were kind and understanding. Well, damn it. She wasn't. She didn't have their patience or forgiveness. Tea was pissed, plain and simple. It appeared that yet again she had to live by other's dictates. The twins could do whatever they wanted, and Tea had to accept their choices if she wanted to stay with them. Emotions went to war inside of her.

Damn. She wasn't a good person.

Anger won the battle even though she worked to keep her emotions in check. The twins didn't even ask her. They didn't give her a chance. She was passed over like that tasteless applesauce. They were hers, and no one had a right to them.

Tea snatched the note out of Duke's pocket and held up the paper. "Who's Rena?"

"A friend, Tea-cup." Baron shrugged. "Don't worry. It's bad for your health."

"Don't lie to me, and stop telling me not to worry." The paper crumpled in her fist.

"It's not a lie." Duke's brow furrowed. "She's someone we perhaps know."

"Perhaps? Probably? Someone?" Tea fumed. "A prostitute you're trying to proposition is simply someone you know? How much are you paying? What does she do for you?"

"Tea, please don't worry—" Baron was interrupted by Duke.

"How do you know that?"

"Rena gets around?" Baron supplied. Duke pinned her with a hard look. She didn't care.

"I was listening at the door when you talked last night. I was going to tell you I wasn't cold and I didn't need a sweater. Of course, now I do since you've been bringing the temp down in the apartment."

"You have?" Baron asked his brother. "I thought the room seemed chilly."

"Dude, I had to keep her covered." Duke didn't sound apologetic. "You should thank me."

She wanted him to say he was sorry. She wanted… well, she wanted a lot of things she couldn't have. Never want what you can't have. *Damn*, she was still a fool.

Baron faced her. "Rena is not someone you need to worry about."

"Like I shouldn't have to worry about not being pregnant?"

"That's what this is probably about." Duke shoved his hands in his pockets. "We were probably going to tell you."

"We were going to tell you, no *probably* about it," Baron spoke up. "We were picking the right time."

Tea's anger doubled. "The right time so you can kick me out? Now that I don't need help, you don't need me here. Is that how this works? Is that the game?"

"What?" Duke's eyebrows drew together so hard they made a 'v' on his forehead. The twins exchanged looks.

"If you want an apology for not telling you about the baby, then we'll give you one." Baron stared at her.

"Is that what you want, Tea? Should we say sorry?" Duke asked. "Say the word."

"You want to know what the word is?" Tea turned away from the twins toward the bedroom. "Fuck you."

The situation all made sense to her now. She'd been fooling herself all along. They never needed her for anything. They helped her because of the baby, but they didn't need her for sex or friendship or love. They didn't need her to eat or sleep or have fun. They didn't want her company.

From the beginning, their routine never changed. Tea was a throw pillow. She wanted their lives to change. She wanted her life to change as well. Tea had hoped to become a better person, to have a new life like Luna said. But in the end, nothing here was different. She was still an unlovable junkyard dog. Somewhere along the way she had thought she was in a relationship. She thought she had value. How foolish could she be?

"Tea," Duke began.

"I'm sorry." She reached for the doorknob to the bedroom. All her anger melted into a dull ache in her chest. "Some dumb part of me thought you were mine," she whispered. "I'm a fool, like Mother said." Tea opened the door. "I thought that one day you would like me."

"Tea, wait," Baron called.

"We can probably—" Duke started, but she held up her hand.

"Timeout." She sighed. "No, don't say anything. This is my fault. I thought we were…" She paused. Whatever she thought was ridiculous. "It's fine. I get it. I'm not pregnant. I can go. I'll be on my own. That's how it was and how it will be again. And we're not dating or…" She didn't have a word for three people. She shook her head. The idea she would have to pack up and leave felt singularly worse than all the times she'd been slapped. And that was a lot of times. "I'm not with you."

Tea entered the bedroom, closed the door, and leaned against the wood. Tears leaked out. She could've kept her mouth shut and let them have sex with whomever they wished. If she'd done that, she wouldn't have created this rift. She also wouldn't have to leave, but she'd spoken up because not saying anything would have killed her. Tea wouldn't have been able to sit silently, especially the moment they came back smelling like sex and another woman.

Moving to the bed, Tea sank down on the blanket. She would pack what she could take tomorrow. Even though it hurt her pride, she would ask the twins for a few HOCs. In her head, she scrolled through all the places she could live along the Equator. She should've left a long time ago. A smart decision would've been to get as far away from the H.S.P.C as she could get right from the start.

Too late for that now.

Curling into a ball on the side of the bed, Tea pictured another home. The problem was no place would be her home without the twins.

The door to the bedroom opened with a swish against the carpet. Tea didn't move. She wrapped her arms tighter around her shins and wished she could disappear. Wishing was dumb, but she did it anyway.

"Leave me alone." Her voice was husky. *Damn*, more tears. She never cried, but the twins brought out honest emotions in buckets.

"We can't leave you alone, Tea-cup," Baron spoke first. "We try and fail."

"We probably need to talk, Tea." Duke's hands rubbed gently on her shoulders. "I mean, I *know* we should." When Duke touched her, the feel of his warm skin was equally worse and better.

"We won't let you leave. No probably about it," Baron said simply. "If you want us to not see Rena, then that's what we'll do. We're sorry we didn't tell you about not being pregnant. Whatever you want us to say, we'll say it."

"I'm sorry, Tea." Duke's hand stilled. "I was probably short with you. I was surprised you heard us. I told you we aren't very good at talking with beautiful women like you. You've every right to know what's going on with your body. We were wrong, Tea. If we keep everything the way it is, will you stay with us? Please?"

Tea sat up and thought about what he said. Duke leaned back where he sat on the bed. Baron stood at the foot.

"I've no right to tell you what to do." She dropped her head into her hands. "I don't want our friendship to be like that. I don't know what to say." Did she want to say that they weren't a match? The problem was— they felt like her Conpar. They felt like even more than that. She yearned for them in a way she'd never wanted anyone or anything.

"You can talk to us." Baron nodded. "We said we're here to help you. We haven't changed our minds. Say what you want, and we can make it happen. Say the word."

"I can ask you to not have sex? What right do I have to do that? I lived with someone making me do things. I wouldn't do that to the two of you, but I can't stay here and watch. This hurts."

"Tea," Duke got up from the bed, "Baron thought to ease the pressure." He shoved his hands into his pockets. "I think the tension is getting to us all."

"We wanted to take the edge off," Baron agreed.

"The edge off?" Her eyes jumped back and forth between the two men.

"It's hard, Tea." Duke reached for his yo-yo.

"Nice choice of words, bro." Baron looked at his feet. "It's difficult to be around you." Baron's eyes popped to hers for a second and then dropped to the floor. "We're sexually attracted to you, and we're doing our best to not touch you. We don't want to make you uncomfortable because we—"

"Can we not talk about this anymore?" Duke wouldn't look at her either. He slapped the yo-yo back down on the dresser. His discomfort at the topic was palpable. Duke wasn't shy normally, and his awkwardness had her thinking more and more about what was going on here.

"Is that why you covered up my dress?" She had misread the situation. "You liked it?"

"That dress was way too sexy." Duke leaned next to the exit like he wanted to inch out of the room. "We couldn't stand it."

"Duke dropped the temp to keep you covered." Now Baron sounded embarrassed. "We should've talked with you, but Duke doesn't like to talk about sex."

"Can we go? Everything is fine, right, Tea?" Duke looked hopeful.

"Everything isn't fine," Baron argued. "I don't want Tea to leave. We tell her all the time to talk to us, to trust us, and now look at what we're doing. We're avoiding what's going on here."

"What's going on here?" Tea thought the sexual attraction was only one-sided. After the kiss, the twins acted like they didn't like her any longer. Now she understood that the boys had the same feelings she did. Her heartbeat picked up at the thought.

"If we promise not to see Rena, could we go back to the way it was?" Duke asked.

"Are you listening to yourself?" Baron faced Duke. "What happened to looking at this from all angles?"

"I am," Duke fired at Baron.

"No, you're not! I don't want to deal with this either, but you know how bad this is becoming. You got a boner watching her cook in the kitchen… I was in surgery. I have to concentrate."

"And I turned the apartment into an ice chest. She was covered. I had it figured out."

"A boner?" Tea stared back and forth between the two of them. "You get hard at the same time?" Suddenly Duke's burnt wrist and the conversation after the closet incident made sense.

Silence.

"Let's forget it." Duke headed toward the door. "I'll toss the letter, and we'll figure something else out. We'll do whatever you want to do, Tea. Just don't leave." His hand was on the doorknob, but it didn't turn. Tea's words stopped him.

"I wanted you to ask me."

Chapter 16

Duke spun around and stared at her. "What did you say?"

"I wanted you to ask me," she repeated. "You said I could ask you for things I wanted. You said to say the word." Tea stood up and gazed at the two men. "I don't want you to ask Rena. I wanted you to ask me. I want to be good enough for you. Be with me."

Baron's eyes went wide. His Adam's apple bobbed.

Tea waited to see what they would say. She'd fought, she'd faced men who wanted to kill her, she survived the H.S.P.C. torturing her, but right now, waiting for them to respond might be more frightening than all those moments combined.

Baron glanced at his brother and then back at her. "You are good enough for us."

"You're better," Duke agreed. "We do want you, but perhaps—"

"I don't want to hear the word perhaps or probably." She sighed.

"It's only that just one of us can't have you. That's not how this works." Baron gave another quick glance at Duke. "We're connected."

"Zap-my-dangles." Duke sat on the bed and buried his head in his hands. "Tell her and get it over with. It's not like I can stop you."

"You could punch me."

"Don't tempt me, dude."

"Tell me what?" Tea looked to Baron when Duke was clearly not going to explain.

"Duke and I—" Baron started.

"—fuck together. We get hard as a pair, and we come as a pair."

Duke got up. "There." He spat at Baron. "Are you happy now? We told her what kind of screwed up lives we live." He wouldn't look at her now. "We're a mess. We fight. We can't have a relationship. I have to have sex with my brother in the room. Everything around us is broken. We break things." Duke tossed his hand out at the beds on the floor. "That's what we have to offer someone. A broken screwed up life."

"Duke, can we talk about this?" Baron asked. "Bro, please."

"No. Forget it."

The silence this time gave Tea time to think. When she first thought about having sex with the twins, she pictured taking turns. One, then the other, then back again. The concept was a fun fantasy, but this new idea was even better. Both of them would be hers at the same time.

Tea wanted to be apologetic about liking the notion, but she wasn't. Sex with a set of hot twins turned her on. There was a chance parts of her darker side might never change completely even if she worked to be a better person and live a better life. It never bothered her that the boys beat each other. When it came to sex with them both, she wanted that. It was perfect.

"You have to be in the same room?" Tea asked to make sure she had this correct.

"I guess forgetting it is out?" Duke muttered.

"We have to be touching." Baron sat on the edge of the bed. "Not like a lot. I don't want to touch my brother, but it must be some piece of skin. We tend to pick our ankles when we jerk off."

"I'm done with this." Duke headed to the door. "I'm going for a walk." She'd never seen Duke shy or uncomfortable before. He was always relaxed and internal.

"Wait," Tea called out before Duke left. Duke didn't turn around, but he stopped with his hand on the doorknob.

"Are you going to ask me?"

"Ask you what?" Duke spun around and shoved his hands into his pockets. He stared at the wall above her head.

"You said you were attracted to me." She looked to Baron for confirmation. "It's hard?"

"Nothing wrong with your memory," Baron shrugged.

"Are you going to ask me to have sex with you?" She looked at Duke since she already had the idea the younger twin wouldn't need persuading. A small grin hung on her lips. This was new to her. Mother basically tossed her in a room with anyone having Cuban blood to see if they were a match. She'd never had to talk to someone about sex, or coax, or seduce before. The twins said they didn't know how to talk to women; well, she didn't know how to talk to a man. In this case, two.

Duke and Baron shared another one of those long looks. They were having a silent conversation. No way would Tea let them keep doing that. This was too important.

"Timeout." Tea held up her hand. "Stop talking to each other. Talk to me."

"We aren't talking," Baron argued. "I never said anything."

"I have eyes." She rubbed her scar as she attempted to come up with the right words. "No silent conversations. Tell me how you feel. Do you want to be with me?"

"We have to tell you how we feel?" Duke asked. "But you don't have to?"

"Low blow, Duke," Baron admonished.

"No." Tea's eyes met Duke's. "He's right." She came to stand at the foot of the mattress. "I like you both. I've wanted you both from the beginning, but I didn't know how to say that. I was afraid if I told you what I wanted to have sex with you both that you'd kick me out." She paused. "But I'm not a shy young girl anymore. If that's an issue, I get it, but I can't change my past. That train left the tracks years ago. I've had sex. Mother used to put me in a room to see if I was a match." Tea's eyes flipped to Baron to see if her experience with men would bother him. "If you want a shy virgin, I'm not it."

"No, it's not that." Baron's brow furrowed. "We—"

Duke didn't finish his brother's sentence. His lips pressed together as he studied the carpet.

"If it's about knowing how to have sex, I know what I'm doing. I'm not scared to be with you as a pair. If you want me, now is the time when you'd have to say the word."

They clearly wanted her, but something was in the way. Something that they weren't sharing with her. They stared at each other in another twin-only conversation.

Well, she would give them a strong nudge. She didn't need her gift for that. Stepping between the two men, she grasped the bottom of her sweater. The twins watched her intently, mute.

"I'll wait here while you decide." With the sweep of her arms, she pulled the large sweatshirt over her head. The top was tossed to the floor. She would raise the temperature of the room, and she didn't need to touch the thermostat.

"I'm going to need a definitive answer."

"I…" Baron looked at Duke.

"If you want to talk about what we can do together." Tea hooked her thumbs into her sweatpants and tugged. The fabric fell easily to the floor. "I want to do that." She stepped out of the pants then faced the bed. "I'd like to know how you feel." She could feel two sets of eyes hungrily roaming her exposed flesh. "I know I don't share what I'm thinking, but I'm okay with two dicks. Unless that's a problem for you?"

"You share when you're half asleep," Duke muttered under his breath.

"A problem?" Baron's eyes bounced everywhere in the room and then landed on her.

"Does it bother you that I've been with other men?"

Both men shook their heads.

"I'm not thinking about that." Baron's eyes made a trail from the dresser back to her body.

"Is it a problem that I used to be with The Originals?"

"We don't hold your past against you, little Tea." Duke's eyes speared hers.

"Then I'm here, and I want you both. Tell me what you like and how you feel." Tea pulled her stretchy bra over her head and tossed the top to the floor. Her breasts bounced free. "I'm saying the word."

"I feel dizzy." Duke breathed.

"What we like?" Baron's Adam's apple bobbed a second time.

"Could one of you move the beds together?" she asked.

Baron moved like he'd just been kicked in the ass. He jumped and shoved the mattresses together like when the guys did yoga.

"Thank you." Tea didn't spare them another glance. She sank to the nearest bed and crawled across the blankets. She settled her butt in the middle and reclined against one of the pillows. Her fingers played with the waistband of her underwear. She couldn't decide if she should take them off yet. Her twins appeared like they'd just been pumped with quarts of the immobilization drug.

Baron moved first. He took one step toward the bed, but Duke grabbed his shirt.

"What do you think you're doing?" Duke gulped.

"I'm going to climb on the bed with Tea." Baron's eyes shot to her and then traveled down to her breasts. They stopped on her white underwear contrasting against her bronze skin. "I'm going to kiss her until *I'm* dizzy."

"We need to think this through. This probably isn't a good idea." Duke's eyes traveled over her body and landed on her underwear. "Isn't this wrong?"

"It's not wrong. I'm inviting you into my bed." Tea tipped her head as she watched them. "Well… it's your bed."

"But you're regular." Duke's nervousness was surprising. Tea was shocked that a naked woman he found appealing didn't override his caution. She didn't even know men like that existed.

"Tea isn't regular. She's amazing," Baron argued.

"I know." Duke looked like he couldn't decide if he should run from the room or follow his brother. "I'm saying Tea is not like Rena. We should think about this. Look at it from all angles."

"I haven't come in seven months, and a beautiful naked woman is on my bed. You think I'm going to sit around and think about this? No. Please, for once in your life don't think and ponder and look at this from all angles. Don't say probably. Just strip naked, and let Tea have us any way she wants." Baron's eyes pleaded with his brother before he glanced at her again. "You want us, right, Tea?"

"Yes."

"Both of us?" Baron shoved Duke's hand off his chest. The younger twin pulled his shirt over his head and threw the top behind him. "And you'll be ours?"

"Yes."

"Both?" Duke's eyes traveled over her body. "Really?"

"Yes," she repeated as she lifted her body and slipped off her underwear. "I've never been with two men, but I like you both. I'd like to be with you together if that's how you do it."

"How do we know you're choosing to do this?" Duke asked her as his eyes strayed to the exit. "I don't want you to trade favors. We won't see a prostitute. We won't look for any other women. You don't have to touch us, Tea."

"But I want to." Tea's eyes went to Baron's pants as she tossed her panties to the floor.

"You want me to take off my pants?" he asked.

"If you're naked, it's easier to have sex." She grinned.

"Ha." Baron pushed his pants down then struggled out of his underwear. He kicked his clothing to the side. "Done."

The younger twin's cock was rock hard. The thick shaft tumbled out of the fabric prison ready for action. His eagerness caused her grin to morph into a wide, full-mouth smile but the sight of a dick that big had her hoping he wasn't too eager. She would need time to get comfortable with something so thick.

"Tea." Baron knelt on the bed next to her. "This is okay?" Gently, he set his hand on her ankle. His fingers rubbed up her calf as if testing if she would push him away. "Duke is right. You don't have to do this. We won't touch anyone. You can stay here and never do…" Baron paused, and his eyes flashed to her breasts with blatant longing. Her nipples tightened. "Us."

"I thought you said, 'say the word' for what I want." Her hand skimmed over her breast, then down her belly. "Word." She combed through the small triangle of hair between her legs. "I'm not a shy virgin, Baron. I know what I'm doing. I'm old enough to know what I'm asking for. I'm not trading favors." Her eyes went to Duke. "I'm not trying to force you into bed with me either." She bit her lip as she made an effort to come up with the right way to explain. "I took off my clothes to offer you an evening with me. You can stay or go. We can do this once and never do it again. You have choices. I have choices." Tea smiled when that truth sank in. "It's amazing to realize I have choices." She was on her own, but this time in a good way. She was at the helm of her life.

"I like it when you smile," Duke whispered more to himself.

"For the love of Pete, decide, bro." Baron's eyes jumped to his brother.

Tea glanced at the door, and she prayed like mad that they wouldn't leave. "I'm going to be right here whether you stay or go."

After a minute, Duke nodded. Baron exhaled.

"I'm going to shower. When I get back, you have to tell us what you want us to do." Duke yanked off his shirt and threw the top to the floor. The muscles of his abs and chest rippled. Tea held her victory smile. "I mean it. I'm not doing this unless you tell us what pleases you, Tea." He glared at Baron. "Not the other way around. If we have sex, then it's going to be about your pleasure, and if you want to stop at any time, we will. I swear if you don't like it, I'll make this pinhead get up and leave this room."

Tea grinned as he unbuttoned his jeans.

"I say what I want, and you deliver?"

"Yes." Duke shoved his pants and underwear to the floor and kicked them to the side. He looked as thick and as swollen as his brother. They were a matching set.

Duke turned away from her and walked to the bathroom. As his hand reached the door, a sudden thought struck her.

"What if you don't want to do what I want to do?" Her eyebrows drew together. "Maybe you won't like it." This talking about sex was way more difficult than being told to have sex by Mother. On the other hand, it was also more exciting, and she felt cared for that they were both eager to make her happy.

Duke paused and looked over his shoulder. She stared at his ass as the muscles flexed. His eyes hungrily devoured her naked frame. Her skin sizzled with that one look.

"I was about to hump an electrical socket the other day watching your ass sway while you cooked in the kitchen." Duke exhaled. "I doubt you'll ask me to do anything I don't want to do, but if Baron or I don't like something, we'll go to the living room."

"No matter what happens, it changes nothing about this living arrangement. We want you here." Baron's hand moved from her knee to her outer thigh. "You can always stay with us, and we'll always help you."

"Then help me. Make me come." She pinned Duke with a look that she hoped conveyed her seriousness.

"I'll be right back." Duke groaned and then turned to the bathroom door. She saw the way his hands shook as he exited the room.

Chapter 17

After Duke disappeared into the bathroom, Tea eyed Baron. His hand ran along her thigh making a lazy pattern.

"Why does he have to shower now? He's throwing off his routine."

"Ha." Baron grinned. "Trust me when I say you've been throwing us off ever since we met you." Baron moved next to her on the bed and brushed a kiss on her shoulder. "Don't worry about Duke. He showers before sex because he thinks women don't like the smell of the metal wires and the soldering iron. His girlfriend told him that."

"Girlfriend? You both had a girlfriend together?" Tea heard the water in the shower hit the walls. She smiled back at Baron as he trailed kisses along her collarbone.

"Not together." Baron's fingers traced her thigh. "Duke and I went our separate ways after our parents died of Snow Flu. I was a real dick about it. I ditched Duke and moved to the Party Base. I stayed high and drunk because I couldn't deal with the pain. I worked shoveling out the animal stalls."

"And what did Duke do?"

"He moved to HQ and got a job as an H.S.P.C. postal clerk. We didn't have our gifts at first, so it didn't matter what we did. While Duke was at headquarters, he met a woman. She broke his heart."

"Is she the reason Duke says he can't talk to women?"

"She messed him up big time. I wasn't there to help him." Baron wrapped an arm around her shoulders. "After Duke and I got our gift and our side effect, she split. She didn't want both of us. Only him and only the way she wanted him. I think she was trying to turn him into something. She always made him shower before sex."

"I don't mind how he smells." She snuggled into Baron's arms. "I like how you smell. It's your shaving lotion."

"You smell like whatever you've been cooking and something else I want to eat." Baron scooted lower on her body and then nuzzled her belly. He inhaled. "While we wait," Baron smiled, "I can entertain you."

Tea laughed. "You can?"

Baron scooped her up into his arms, and she squeaked in surprise. He sat against the wall and then settled her so that she straddled his lap. They faced each other. His erection nestled between her legs and pressed against her stomach warm and solid.

Tea rocked against the proud shaft. Her mound pressed lovingly to what would soon be inside of her. He sucked in a deep breath. His eyes became a smoky indigo as she shifted against him repeatedly. Slowly, he brought his mouth to hers and kissed her until she was out of breath. The taste of him was exactly like before. There was a mix of urgency and sweetness.

"I can juggle."

Tea laughed. "You can entertain me with juggling later." Tea's eyes studied his handsome face, and then she heard the water click off. The silence of the room started to steal her confidence.

"What's wrong?" Baron asked as he rubbed her stiff shoulders.

"Maybe Duke doesn't want to do this. Am I making him? I don't want to force anyone into anything. I'm not like Mother."

"No. Duke wants you, Tea. That was the fastest shower Duke has ever taken. This isn't only my hard-on, Tea-cup. This is his too." Baron dipped his head and trailed kisses along her jaw to her ear. "You've been the only thing on our minds for weeks. Duke wants you, but when it comes to sex, he's shy."

"He isn't shy anywhere else. The first time I met him, he pissed in front of me."

"I think the first reason he's bashful is that he has to put up with me being here. Duke doesn't like having sex with me in the room. He never lets me jerk off. I think it's one of the reasons we fight so much."

"That's the first reason? What's the second?"

"I think the second is he doesn't want to scare you away with what he likes in the bedroom."

Baron's words intrigued her. "What does he like that's so scary?"

"We'll do whatever you want to do, Tea. Not the other way around." Baron's tongue traced her collarbone. "I can't tell you how happy I am to have you in my arms. I'm not going to make a mistake and have you leave."

"You're not going to make a mistake. I'm not a fragile little teacup and I'm not leaving." Tea gripped Baron's cock between them and started a slow up and down sliding of her hand until Baron wiggled his hips. "I have preferences that you might not like too. It's okay if we talk about them. Just because we talk doesn't mean we have to do them."

"Whatever you want, say the word." Baron groaned when her hand closed over the tip of his erection and then slipped back down. Pre-cum made her fingers slippery as she circled the head. Baron gasped.

"What does Duke like to do?" she whispered and then licked her fingers. Baron shuddered.

"Okay." Baron gave a quick glance to the door. "Don't tell Duke I told you, but he's into anal sex and blowjobs. Those are his favorite. I know because that's what he pays for when we can afford a prostitute."

"I don't understand."

"Me neither. I like to eat pussy." Baron's mouth dipped to her chest. "And nipples like yours make my mouth water."

"That's not what I meant." She squirmed when Baron sucked one of her nipples into his mouth. She moaned, and Baron lifted his head. "I mean, I don't understand why you pay for sex. You're both handsome and smart and fun. Why don't you have a girlfriend?"

"For—"

"—a lot of reasons." Duke's voice cut into the conversation as he came out of the bathroom. "The fighting scares women. The arguing, the brawls, the blood. The joint sex isn't normally okay either. We've been called gross and that it's incest. Even hookers don't like it."

"Even if we explain that it's attached to our gifts, they don't care." Baron's hands traced the underside of her breasts. "They gossip about us."

"And we've never met a regular woman who likes us both." Duke stood next to the bed with a towel around his waist. "They normally like one of us and hate the other. That always happens." His hair was damp, but his skin was dry. The creamy-white skin had a slight pink tint to the pale contours. Tea assumed he showered in extremely hot water.

"I like you both. Your fighting doesn't scare me, but if we have sex, maybe I'll tire you out." Tea slipped off Baron's lap and inched until she was at the edge of the mattress kneeling in front of Duke. She tugged on Duke's towel until the terrycloth fell to the floor. Her eyes stayed fixed on his face.

"I'll try that," Baron groaned behind her. "Yoga isn't working."

Duke's erection was still as hard as his brother's, and he stood next to the bed like he wasn't sure what he should do next. He didn't cover himself, but his eyes dropped to his dick like he wished he had pockets.

"Are you staying here with us now?" Tea reached out and slipped her fingers over Duke's cock.

"I'll stay until you say the word." His eyes closed.

"I hope I'll be so busy screaming with your cock inside of me that I won't be saying anything." Tea worked her hand over Duke's shaft.

Duke visibly shook at her sentence. She grinned. Saying something even remotely dirty got to the older twin. She would have to remember that for the future.

Dropping to his knees, Duke moved to kiss her lips. His big hands closed over her breasts, and she gasped at the rough contact. His mouth continued to kiss and then lick.

Baron got up and left the bed, but she didn't have time to ask where he went. Duke's mouth and hands skimmed all over her. He seemed hungry for her as he ran his fingers along her skin as if he memorized her for the future.

"This is okay?" Duke lifted his mouth from hers.

"Yes."

When Duke let go of her, she wiggled until she rested in the center of the bed. Tea pressed her back flat in the middle of the blanket. Her eyes studied Duke as she waited to see what he would do next.

After a few seconds, Duke crawled over to her side. His cock, hard and begging, hovered near her left breast. When Baron returned, the younger twin moved between her legs and knelt on all fours. He set a tube next to her knee, and then his hands slipped over her. His fingers danced from her calves, to the curve of her ass, then to her inner thighs. Baron spread her legs. His breath was warm on her skin where the air brushed her knee. When his mouth descended, she arched her back.

Duke's hard shaft jumped proudly for attention. Without thought, she ran her hand over the velvety skin. His breath hitched as he rocked into the sure strokes of her palm over the head. Groaning, Tea relished the feel of him heavy and solid against her fingers. His hard-on curved upward slightly past his belly button. Tea kept pumping over him and Duke trembled. She wanted to taste both her twins, but tonight she might not get the chance. The feel of them moving inside her body was simply too seductive.

Desire that she'd been keeping at bay suddenly bloomed. Already she was wet, and as Baron pushed her legs even further apart, she was sure he could smell the scent of her arousal. Tea was so ready for this. Her fantasy did nothing to compare to real life.

Tea pulled her hand away from Duke's erection. As Duke scooted close, his cock left a trail of pre-cum along her skin. She turned her head toward his thick shaft. When her mouth reached the older twins' member, she licked the tip.

Duke groaned.

"You want me to keep going?" She ran her tongue over Duke again as she twisted ever so slightly toward his beckoning shaft. Baron sprinkled kisses on her thighs.

"Whatever you want." Duke's hips rocked toward her.

Baron adjusted closer. As his tongue made a leisurely trip to land on her clit, she forgot to respond to Duke. The younger twin sucked on her slit like he wanted every drop of cream from her body.

"Baron." She wiggled. If he kept doing that, she would come in a second.

"Stop?" Duke asked.

"No. Don't stop." She panted. "It's only that Baron will make me come if he keeps going."

"Ha." Baron laughed lightly next to her wet skin. "I promised to entertain."

"You're so hot, little Tea." Duke's thumb slipped over her nipples until they pebbled to hardened points. One hand moved lower until his fingers circled her belly button. Where their skin touched left a zing of pleasure.

The cool air of the bedroom passed over her rapidly heating skin. Victory that she would soon have the twins soared inside of her. They would be hers now. This is what a Conpar wanted. No. This is what a real match yearned to have forever. Her channel rippled and squeezed waiting for them.

Baron dipped his head and ran his tongue easily over her sensitive wet flesh. Her hips rose off the blanket.

Tea turned her head back toward Duke's erection as Baron began to suck on the little swollen nub that gave her so much pleasure. When the younger twin said he liked pussy, he clearly meant it. He lapped at her like he was in heaven. Tea wrapped her hand around Duke's cock and licked the swollen crown just so she wouldn't orgasm right away. The older twin gave one sharp gasp of surprise before he started a rhythm swaying into her mouth. Duke's cock teased her lips, and he gripped her hair. She concentrated on that. The more possessive side of him fueled the desire building inside of her.

Baron's tongue drilled into her wet lips lapping and sucking at the juices. She moaned as her other hand grabbed the back of Baron's head. Her fingers fisted into his hair so he couldn't lift his mouth away. She kept pumping Duke's shaft as she inched closer and closer to her release.

Neither twin seemed interested in leaving her anytime soon. Baron sucked and drew her clit into his mouth. Tingles raced over her skin. Her thighs locked as she headed straight for a powerful climax. She sucked hard on Duke's cock memorizing the feel of him on her tongue.

"I'm going to come," she moaned as she pulled her mouth away from Duke. She couldn't catch her breath.

"I want to watch." Duke's voice was a heavy pant. His cock slipped out of her hand as he sat back on his heels next to her. Tea shuddered and shook, and then she flew. An extraordinary orgasm crashed through her with astonishing strength and unbelievable power.

As Tea floated down from the waves of pleasure, Baron's breath washed over her navel. He pulled himself up on the bed to her right side. After relaxing flat on his back on the blanket, he reached for her. Tugging her into his arms, the younger twin set her on top of him. She could feel his dick hard and hot against her clit. He didn't enter her, but simply held her, chest to chest. He kissed her shoulder and neck before burying his face in her hair. As he inhaled, he ground against her body like he couldn't help it. She was still freefalling as Baron's fingers squeezed between their bodies and rubbed over her clit lovingly. The climax overwhelmed her, and she strained to grab oxygen as he kept her body from rippling with ecstasy a second time. Baron kissed her and inhaled every moan that slipped past her lips.

When the moment of euphoria lifted, she wiggled on top of Baron and sat upright. Baron watched her intently as she took a few calming breaths.

"You're still hard." She shifted on Baron and glanced at Duke. The older twin moved behind her and knelt between Baron's legs. She straddled Baron's lap but tipped forward slightly. Duke's eyes dropped to her ass.

"Yes," Baron agreed.

"We both are," Duke muttered. "We come at the same time."

"You want to come inside of my ass?" Tea looked over her shoulder at Duke. His eyes still drilled into her backside.

"Tea, I don't even know what to say to something like that." Duke trembled as his eyes popped to hers.

"Yes or no are the words in this situation."

"Yes. I want anything you want to do." Duke pressed closer and wrapped his arm around her waist. His cock trailed pre-cum along her ass cheeks.

Tea smiled. Duke might have a thing for talking dirty. She shifted backward until Duke's cock rubbed up and down her crack. Her fingers went to her wetness and stroked her lips before trailing the juices to her anus. She'd done this before. There was always something about the fullness she loved. Having anal sex and being tougher than the man she was with always made the sex better. Now, there was nothing about this sex that she could consider as better.

"Tea," Duke groaned.

"Stop?"

"No. This is so hot," came Duke's gruff answer. Duke had a bit of a dark side. One she would delight in exploring.

Baron moved impatiently under her and shifted his dick between her legs. His fingers danced over her chest and nipples. His stunning blue eyes, darkening with desire, caught hers. The younger twin's mouth followed his hands. The touch of his tongue on her skin fed the fire inside of her soul. Tea struggled to move, but Duke's grip around her waist stopped that from happening.

"I've wanted to do this since I kissed you," Duke whispered before his mouth traveled over her shoulders. His lips trailed down her back, then along her spine. Duke never let go of her, but moved his grip to her thighs as he sprinkled kissed all the way to her ass. The older twin moved from cheek to cheek before his tongue serpentined toward her hole. Tea was completely shocked as Duke licked greedily at her flesh. She bent forward onto Baron's hard chest. She squirmed. Her heart pounded as she held her breath. Duke's tongue rimmed her anus, and then she felt him adjust himself behind her.

Duke had one hand gripping her thigh as Baron tipped her chin to line up their lips. The younger twin kissed her over and over again as if perfectly happy to be underneath her while he waited for what Duke would do next. Baron caressed her chest, then belly. His hands skimmed everywhere as his mouth made her dazed. When his lips lifted from hers, his intense stare surveyed her flushed face.

"You like being on top of me?" Baron asked.

"Yes," she panted.

"And you like Duke behind you?"

"Yes, but I'm going out of my mind waiting. I know I should say the word, but I have no idea what that word is."

"Ha." Baron grinned. "I don't know what the word is either."

Duke's rumbling laugh came from behind her ass cheeks. "I'm looking at you from all angles. I probably have to think this through."

Suddenly, Duke's fingers rubbed between Tea's ass cheeks. She heard the slippery wetness of lube and a growl of approval from Duke. Again, Duke's hand ran down the side of her thigh, but this time Tea didn't mind the wait. When she felt the first gentle pressure of his fingers, her eyes closed.

First, there was one finger and then two. The digits slipped into her backside. She whimpered while she tried in vain to adjust Baron's hard cock into her body. She tried desperately to move, but Duke wasn't letting that happen. Duke held her thighs, and Baron lifted his head up to suck on her nipples. She was trapped between the two men, but in a good way.

Lost in the feel of Duke's hands, she was disappointed when his fingers disappeared. Instantly, Baron lifted her and glided her down to engulf his thick erection. Tea felt every inch of him slide inside of her.

"Yes," Baron groaned as his eyes closed. "I'm never going to last."

"You better last," Duke muttered.

As soon as Baron's thickness settled all the way inside of her, Duke replaced his hands with his pulsating flesh.

"This is…" Duke's length rimmed her hole, and then there was pressure when his massive erection pressed against the tight ring of muscle. "Yes?"

"Yes," Tea moaned.

Baron took that moment to lift his hips and press his cock deeper before letting an inch of the hard length slide out of her.

"Yeah, that feels amazing." Baron arched his back.

A moan of pure ecstasy escaped from between Tea's lips. The sound was all she could do. There was only more pressure and then a stretching burning as Duke pushed further into her body.

Some unfamiliar tickling heat began to infuse her limbs. She felt like liquid fire floating between two magnificent electric connections. Her body sizzled with pain and then pleasure. There was so much pleasure she couldn't take it all in.

"If you want me to stop, you have to say it," Duke whispered behind her. "Say it. Say you want this." His voice sounded far away. His words overflowed with anguish like pulling out of Tea would kill him.

"I want you both," Tea gasped. The feeling of both men was so all-encompassing she could hardly put those four words together. Duke's hard cock and the hard muscles of his body molded to Tea's back. They made her tremble with deep longing. She wouldn't deny Duke anything, not that she wanted to. She wanted Duke to move deeper inside of her and feel Baron's erection massaging her inner walls like he belonged there.

"Slide into me," Tea pleaded. "I need to feel you both moving." Tea hoped Duke would understand how much she wanted this. It was no longer about another woman or about fear of being kicked out. This moment with the twins had turned into a need, a craving fiercer than anything she'd ever felt before. Tea didn't know that being with both these men would be a mixture of pleasure, pain, and a concentrated connection so powerful she couldn't escape. She would never want to leave Duke or Baron, no matter what happened next.

Duke's cock still moved into her like there was no end to its size. There was pressure and then a sting which gave way to a fullness that swept her closer to climax. At first, she tried to pull away from the building force, but Duke held her hips. The sensation was a slow-building ecstasy and a burn mixing together.

Slowly, Duke thrust shallowly in and out of her ass. Tea's eyes closed as her body relaxed into him. The older twin wrapped an arm around her waist and kissed her shoulders and the back of her neck. He held her as he directed Baron to move in and out of Tea's throbbing slit. Her hips rocked, beginning a light, leisurely sway between both men. Her tight canal gripped Baron's throbbing head as her body begged for orgasm.

"I need more," she pleaded.

"Whatever you want, Tea," Baron rasped.

"Say the word." Duke's breath slithered along her shoulder.

"Word."

Baron returned to caressing her hypersensitive skin. Everything was overly sensitized. The continued saturation and the deliberately easing pace made her head spin.

Right when she thought she would beg Duke to make the sweet torment end, Duke froze. The older twin grabbed her thighs. Tea could only get out a moan to describe the feel of the exquisite tenderness. Duke flexed his hips hard. The final spearing made her feel full to bursting. Her entire body screamed to climax. All she wanted was for Duke to pound in and out until she released.

"Relax, little Tea," Duke murmured into her ear. "You've got all of me, and we'll move slow, right Baron?"

"Yes," Baron murmured his agreement. Tea pressed down on Baron's hard shaft snuggled deep inside of her wet slit. The older twin began to guide his cock to thrust in and out of Tea's body more deeply now. As he moved, too many consuming sensations devoured her.

No longer was Tea attached to her body. Now she connected to Duke and Baron like they were all one being. She drifted back and forth between them as her second orgasm built. The friction in her ass had her pleasure climbing to new heights. Duke whispered something about not stopping. The older twin moved harder and harder as her ass absorbed the complete penetration. Every time Duke's cock slid part way out, her channel fisted tightly on Baron.

"Don't stop," she screamed. Tea bucked to force both cocks faster inside of her. Duke set a relentless rhythm. In and out was all she could fit into her brain.

Duke's mouth sucked at the side of her neck. Delicately he rained kisses over her cheek to the back of her ear. Baron's hands returned to her nipples. He muttered her name as his thumb found her clit.

"I'm going to come." Duke's words came out as a half-moan declaration.

Baron gripped her thighs trying to get deeper inside of her body. He lifted his head and latched onto her nipple.

"Say it, Tea. Say that you want us to come inside of you. Say something," Duke begged.

Tea reached for her voice. With all the emotions surging inside of her, she could hardly put a thought together.

"Duke, fill me. Baron, move, please. Oh God, I love you, both." The affirmation was out of her mouth before she could stop it, but she didn't care. Tea absorbed the moment of love and ecstasy.

"Yes, Tea." Duke drove into her harder as Baron's fingers slid over her clit in a demand that she come with them.

"Tea," Baron called out. "Come for us."

Tea's orgasm reached a fevered pitch. Baron pumped his hips and groaned her name. She squeezed and milked Baron's dick. Stars burst in front of her closed eyes as her whole body was branded by these two men. She exploded into a thousand pieces.

Duke pushed her forward onto Baron's chest. Tea ground mercilessly on Baron's shaft as the younger twin thrust deep. She couldn't escape all the feelings surrounding her and filling her. Tea's clit swelled as her back passage filled with hot, liquid heat from Duke.

Letting go of her thighs, Duke's strong hands moved to caresses her lower back as the older twin came inside of her. Her orgasm was so powerful she felt like she was riding the sun into infinite space. Tea swam in currents of heat and couldn't gather enough energy to roll off of Baron's chest. The only thing she felt was Duke's careful withdrawal from her body, and the loss of Baron from her wet center.

Both twins gingerly set her on the bed next to Baron. Her body was boneless. She'd been melted by the heat. Tea's pounding heart was the only reason she was sure she'd not died and gone to heaven. Her entire body pulsed with pleasure. Baron panted as he stared at the ceiling next to her. She snuggled closer to him and set her head on his arm.

Vaguely, she heard Duke in the bathroom. The bed dipped when he returned. The older twin pulled Tea into his arms, and she fell asleep between the two men she loved.

Chapter 18

"Baron?"

Tea didn't recognize the voice that woke her from her dreamless slumber. The stern exasperated call wasn't Duke. Her eyes fluttered open. They alighted on Doctor Mather. Baron's friend stood at the foot of the beds.

As she sat up, Tea yanked the sheet to cover her chest. Her eyes jumped around the room. The blankets clutched to her breasts uncovered a completely naked Duke on her right. Hers and Doctor Mather's eyes met. She bit her bottom lip to stop from screaming. *Damn, stay calm.*

"Baron?" She didn't bother whispering. She elbowed Baron's shoulder.

"Yes, my Tea-cup," Baron whispered happily and snuggled closer to her. His hand snaked around her waist. She shoved him. One of Doctor Mather's dark eyebrows rose.

"You must've stayed up late," Mather threw out conversationally. Tea bit her lip to stop from either panicking or laughing. Whichever. Yes, staying up late was an understatement. They'd stayed up until a few hours ago. Her ass was feeling it.

"Is he late for work?"

"Yes," Mather said slowly.

"Baron," she said his name louder. This time her sharp command woke Duke. His eyes fluttered open. He spotted her and kissed her shoulder before he glanced around the room.

Tea knew the second Duke's eyes landed on Mather.

"Zap-my-dangles." Duke hopped to his feet. He didn't have anywhere to go with the bed pushed against the wall. As soon as he stood, his eyes dropped to his dick, then flipped to Mather. Quickly, he bent down and picked up his pillow. He held the white fluff between his legs.

"Baron, get your ass up," Duke commanded. "Now, dude."

"What, bro?" Baron opened one eye. "You're not even hard." He noted his brother standing on the bed, and then he glanced at her. Tea could also tell the moment Baron spotted Doctor Mather.

"Mather." Baron's booming exclamation was followed by him rising. Just like Duke, it appeared to her that it came to Baron a little late that he was naked. Baron did the same thing his twin had done. He grabbed a pillow and held the mass over his groin. "This isn't—" Baron began.

"—what it looks like." Duke finished.

"You're not sleeping in and missing work?" Mather looked like he might laugh. His eyes dropped to hers. Tea decided to keep her cool. The boys weren't doing a very good job, so it was up to her. If she acted as if she belonged here maybe she wouldn't give Doctor Mather any reason to question her presence.

"I'm sorry that Baron is late for work," Tea said more calmly then she felt. "It won't happen again."

"For the love of Pete! Work. I'll be there in a second." Baron hopped off the bed and then he stopped and stared at the doctor. After a second, he glanced at his brother. "Duke we need to talk."

"One minute, Mather." Both Duke and Baron turned away from the doctor and rushed to the closet. They talked in low tones, and she guessed they dressed. While she found the pillow outfits sexy as hell, she didn't think Mather thought they were cute.

Mather's scanned her, and she swallowed hard. Hopefully, the twins would hurry.

"I take it you overdosed on pills?"

Tea thought fast. "I wanted the twins' attention. It was reckless and childish." She arranged her sheet tighter around her naked breast and hoped that was an acceptable response.

"Did Baron take good care of you?" The doctor sat down at the foot of the bed. "He's still learning." The twins still talked in the closet in hushed tones. What the hell was taking them so long?

"Baron and Duke helped me." She smiled at the words.

"You like to cook?" Mather asked as he glanced at the closet.

"Yes."

"I have to admit I feel better knowing they took a bath with a pretty woman." Mather rubbed his forehead. "Why not tell me?"

"Connecting with someone and starting a new relationship is hard enough, and with the three of us it's...?" Tea searched for the right word.

"Complex," Baron finished for her. The younger twin appeared out of the closet dressed in navy-blue scrubs that matched his eyes.

"I understand. My brother has two matches." Mather shrugged.

"I'm sorry I'm late." As Baron glanced at Mather, he smoothed down his top. "Thanks for waking me. We can head to the hospital."

Duke leaned in the closet doorway wearing khakis and a yellow shirt. He fiddled with his clothing.

"Doctor Mather, we'd like to keep it quiet that Tea is with us. Three people are different, and we're twins, and already everyone doesn't like us."

"I don't want to hear any more incest jokes." Baron's eyes flipped from Duke to Mather. "We don't need any more gossip."

"I get it." The doctor smiled. "In fact, I'd give you the day off, Baron, but we have that one surgery that we can't miss."

"I know," Baron groaned.

"I have someone covering for us this morning, but maybe you could have free time this afternoon. We can check."

"Thanks." Baron grinned. "Can I have a few more minutes with Tea?"

"Sure. I only stopped here to make sure you were alright. With all the strange things going on, I wanted to know that you and Duke were fine. I didn't mean to interrupt. I can see you in a little bit."

"I appreciate you making sure I was okay." Baron glanced at her and then Duke.

"But you won't tell anyone that Tea is here, right?" Duke's voice was thick with fear, but Tea had a good feeling about Mather. They might be able to keep hiding her. If not, they would deal with that problem when it showed up. Tea could ask the twins to move.

"I don't see why not." Mather headed to the exit.

"Thanks." Duke shuffled closer to her. "We want to keep to ourselves."

"I get it if you want to take things slow. If that's what you need, then I can do that. I'm glad that some of what happened makes sense."

"Thank you." Baron sighed with relief.

Mather reached the door handle and smiled. "Just to be sure, I assume you don't want to dress as a woman?"

"Yes." Baron grinned.

"Just checking."

As soon as the doctor left, Baron scooped her up in his arms and kissed her.

"Good morning, Tea-cup." He dropped his head to her shoulder and nuzzled her neck.

"Stop that." Duke shoved his hands into his pockets. "Last night might've been a one-time thing, and we should talk about it and probably look at this from all angles. I told you that. We can't dive in headfirst without thinking."

Baron ignored Duke and kissed her lips. She sighed into his mouth.

When she lifted her head away from Baron, she noted Duke still stood next to the closet. He looked like he was at a loss for what to do next.

Tea wiggled out of Baron's arms and dropped her sheet. Duke swallowed hard as she stepped directly in front of him. Wrapping her arms around Duke's neck, she kissed him. At first, Duke didn't respond, but then his arms circled her and spread along her back. He pressed her naked body to him as he deepened the kiss. His hands dug into her ass. When he lifted his head, he looked bemused.

"Was last night a onetime only thing between us?" she asked.

Duke shook his head.

"No." Baron ran his hand up and down her spine.

"I didn't think so." She tugged out of their embrace. "I'm going to take a shower. I'll be out to make breakfast in a minute. I'll see you tonight, Baron."

"Wait," Baron called before she left the room.

"What?"

"Would it be okay if I looked at your ass?"

"You both looked at it plenty last night." Tea laughed. "I'm tougher then I look. I feel great. I promise."

"At least take a warm bath and use the medicated ointment on any part of you that's sore." Baron shot a glare at Duke. "You were too hard on her last night."

"She said yes. I asked." Duke glared at his brother.

"Remember what we talked about."

"What do you think I am, a monster?"

"You look like one."

"Timeout. I wasn't complaining." Tea intruded. "I had a great time last night. Stop worrying. It's bad for your health."

"Ha." Baron laughed. "One more thing, before I go to work…"

Duke shoved his hands into his pockets as he stared at her breasts.

"What?" She leaned against the door frame to the bathroom and grinned.

Baron stepped in front of her naked body and growled at Duke. "No getting hard today. I mean it. I've got surgeries that I can't miss. Don't be thinking about last night until I get home."

"Fine." Duke's eyes widened. "I'll hang out in the storage room. I'll think about batteries."

"I'll cook and not hang out with Duke too much."

"Thank you." Baron spun around and kissed her on the nose; then his mouth claimed hers again. After he lifted his head, he stared into her eyes. "Thank you for last night,

Tea. It was the best night of my life." He kissed her cheek. "And today is going to be the longest day ever."

"You'll probably be fine." Duke shrugged.

"Ha." Baron laughed. "Probably."

Chapter 19

The day dragged on. By midafternoon, the day became the longest ever in Tea's life. Baron's prediction had come true.

To keep her mind off the twins, Tea threw herself into her cooking. Baron told her there had been trees planted everywhere in all the community gardens and the underground parks. At the start, people didn't realize they were all apple trees. Now they produced more apples than everyone on the base could eat. Even when they shipped the apples out, there were still leftovers.

Since there was an abundance of apples on Water Base Cure, it was apple pie she baked.

Tea rolled out the dough and finished the crust. Duke's oversized sweater was dusted white like she'd just made love to the flour container. Apple mush clung to the center of the fabric. Tea decided she would have to clean up before Baron came home and before Duke came out of the storeroom. She was a mess.

As she slipped her pie into the oven, the door to the workroom opened, and Duke's massive frame filled the entrance. His eyes roamed over her. She nervously swiped at her forehead leaving a white streak in her hair.

"I…" Duke stared then he cleared his throat. "Hungry."

"We aren't supposed to hang out. You wouldn't want to get hard."

"Nothing wrong with your memory."

"Not that I could make you hard with me simply standing here in a messy hoodie." Her eyes roamed over his hands. She pictured where they had traveled over her skin last night.

"Yes, you could." He smiled before his eyes dropped to the wire he twirled in his fingers. Tossing the wire on the table by the door, he crossed to the kitchen and opened the fridge.

An uncomfortable silence nudged her into speaking.

"I don't know what to do now." She stared at his back. "I've never talked or spent any time with anyone that I've had sex with before. Should I go to the bedroom?"

"I don't know what to do either, but I feel like if you walk away it's going to make this weird." Duke dipped his head into the fridge. "We can just talk like normal." After a few seconds, he pulled out a bowl of leftover vegetables that Tea had prepared last night.

"What did you and your girlfriend talk about after sex?" She dusted the flour off her sweater making a cloud puff around her face.

"All the things I did wrong." Duke hunted in the drawer for a fork.

"I can see why you wouldn't want that joker around." This woman sounded like a real bitch. If Tea ever met her, it wouldn't be pretty, gift or not.

"I didn't break up with her. She left me. I thought dating her was better than being alone."

"You have Baron. It's not like you're ever alone."

"It wasn't like that at first.

"What do you mean?"

"This time, I can explain that." Duke grinned and took a seat at the counter. "Baron was on the Party Base, and I was alone working as a postal clerk. Every water base has a group of H.S.P.C. messengers. The couriers are mostly retired agents or guys that didn't make the cut. I was sorting notes and getting the letters to the correct agents so that they could deliver them. It was lonely work. I like doing stuff by myself, but I was too alone if that makes sense."

"Sure." Tea perched on the stool next to him. "Is that when you decided to find your brother and live together?"

"God no. It all happened so fast. One day I was working, and the next morning I woke up blind." Duke speared a piece of broccoli.

"What happened?"

"I didn't know. I panicked. It was my girlfriend who said we should talk to the doctors on the upper floors of headquarters. As soon as I asked around, I met this strange doctor who had a pet monkey. That dude was an oddball, but people said he was a genius."

"He must be a genius. He gave you your vision back."

"Not exactly. After I talked to the doctor, he said the answer was Baron. I wasn't happy about that. I didn't want to see my brother. I felt like he deserted me after our parents died. He left me to handle the End-Of-Life ceremony, the bodies, all their stuff, and clean out our apartment. I was still pissed, but the doc said I had to see him." Duke set the bowl on the counter and leaned back lost in thought.

"Baron came to headquarters to see you?"

"Yes." Duke shoved veggies into his mouth. He spoke around bites. "The thing is he'd gone blind too. He'd been trying to figure out what happened. He thought it was the drinking and the drugs."

"Was the doctor, right? Did Baron fix everything?"

"When he showed up, our vision came back but with our gifts. The second after we were in the same room together, our vision returned. When it came back, I could see electricity. Baron had microscopic vision. Of course, it came with side effects." Duke finished eating and rose. He went around to the opposite side of the kitchen island.

"The sex." She figured out they didn't love to do that together. They treated the connection like a necessary evil.

"But that wasn't the worst thing. Baron and I can't be apart. We can only go seven hours until we go blind." Duke began washing out his bowl in the sink.

"I take it that your girlfriend didn't like all these changes."

"None of us did. It was a lot for Baron and me to take in. Our lives changed overnight. We got new jobs, and we had to spend time together. I hated that I couldn't even masturbate alone." Drying his hands, Duke didn't look at her and instead put the dish away in the cupboard.

"And your girlfriend left." Tea rose from her stool and came around the counter to stand next to him. After she took his fork away and set the utensil aside, their fingers intertwined.

"At the time, I thought Baron drove her away, but after a while I realized she hated him and he's with me. I'm with him. There's nothing we can do about this." His eyes captured hers. Those twin blue jewels said more than just those words. She understood. Duke was asking for forgiveness for the way his life was, but he didn't need to. Not with her.

Tea moved between his legs. She hugged him. His acceptance was humbling and insightful. The twins didn't love how their lives turned out, but they did their best. She wanted to be like them. She wanted acceptance. What did Luna say? Tea could find peace, love, and forgiveness in her next life. That's what the twins had.

She lifted her head from his chest and their eyes met. He wrapped an arm around her shoulders. They were good men, handsome, smart, and caring. That woman was a fool. She missed out. But Tea wouldn't.

"What's that look for?"

"Her loss, my gain."

Duke grinned as his hands went to her ass. Before she could ask him what he was doing, he scooped her up in his arms. He set her down on the counter right in the middle of the flour dusting the marble counter.

His mouth claimed hers before she could complain. He kissed her softly and then lifted his head.

"We told Baron we wouldn't do this. You told him you wouldn't get hard."

"I don't know where he is right now, but I'm pretty sure this is his hard-on," Duke addressed his pants. "I was talking about my ex-girlfriend. Not a sexy topic."

"What happens if we have sex and Baron isn't here?'

"You come."

"And you don't?"

"I don't care." Duke's eyebrows rose. "Unless you do."

"Are you sure this isn't going to screw up Baron's work?"

Duke gripped the bottom of her sweatshirt and pulled the top over her head. He exposed her breasts.

"I'm not thinking about all the things that could happen." His mouth descended on hers again. His lips sipped, then switched to deep-drugged kisses. She pushed his shirt up to find warm, taut skin. Her hands ran up and down his back.

"You want to fuck me? Make me scream for you?" Tea walked her fingers to his belly and then undid the buttons on his jeans.

"Damn, that's hot." Duke dragged his shirt off, and she snuggled against him. Her tongue absorbed his flavor. The smell of metal and safety beat at her senses.

"I should shower." Duke stood away from the counter and began to strip. He was naked so fast she wondered if stripping was another gift he had.

"Don't shower. Come here and let me feel you deep inside of me."

Duke shook. He stood in the kitchen, hard and trembling. She loved how her words got to him. The expression on his face told her he didn't want to shower. It was obvious he didn't want to wait for his brother, either.

"When you say that kind of stuff, you make me want to do whatever you want."

"You won't come." She eyed his naked frame. She wondered if that was still okay with him.

"I don't care." He reached for her, and his scarred, rough hands went to her sweatpants. He pulled them off. Her panties went next.

Centering himself between her legs, he guided her to the very edge of the counter. His mouth dropped to her breasts. His cock slipped inside of her as if he belonged there.

Duke's mouth found her nipple as he settled deeper into her body. He licked then sucked. He teased until she squirmed on the end of the counter.

"Move." She gasped. "Fuck me, Duke, deep and hard. Make me think about nothing but you."

Duke lifted his head. He smiled at her, and she grinned back.

"You know that gets to me."

"Yes, I do." Her body shamelessly wiggled against him. Her legs wrapped around his waist.

Slowly, Duke finally started to rock his hips. Each measured thrust took him deeper. Both the twins had this way of moving deep inside of her heart. His hands reached up to tunnel into her hair. His mouth dropped to hers again. Tea dug her fingers to the marble counter as he slowly built her climax. Every nerve ending, every impulse was centered on the growing heat between her legs. He took her higher and higher. His groan fueled her hunger.

"More, Duke. Fill me." Pleasure seized her. Tea sucked on his lips. Suddenly, the sensation skyrocketed and burst through her body. Her channel clenched hard on Duke's shaft, and she ripped her mouth away from his as she screamed. "Yes, so good."

"Tea." Duke's body began to shake.

"Yes. You feel so amazing. I can't even think. I just feel you." Tea couldn't concentrate anymore. Spasm after spasm of intense emotions and pleasure hurtled through her body. Each time she came down from the heavens, fresh tremors racked her frame.

Duke kissed her and stayed in her arms, panting. After a few minutes, he lifted his eyes and met hers.

"Tea, that was…" he began. "I…"

"For the love of Pete." Baron's voice cut off Duke. "I told you not to touch her while I was in surgery."

"I was…" Duke visibility gulped. "Sorry," he stammered. "It's that I…" He still stood naked in her arms, shaking. He seemed rooted to the spot. Duke's arms held her waist.

"Whatever, bro. It's no big deal." Baron threw off his coat then stripped off his shirt. "I can join in. It's good you only now got hard. I just finished work ten minutes ago." Baron's hands went to the drawstrings tucked into his scrubs. "I told Mather I had a date." He grinned at her. "I ran back here as fast as I could."

There was something wrong. Tea could tell. Duke stood motionless between her legs. His face was swathed in concentration.

"What's wrong?" Baron stopped tugging at the waist of his pants and marched toward the counter.

Duke finally stepped back from her body. "I, ah, came... already." His brow rippled in confusion. He glanced down at his softening penis. His eyes then popped to her perplexed face.

Tea felt like she'd made some kind of monumental change, but she didn't mean to do anything.

Baron glanced at his brother's body and then looked at the crotch of his pants. The outline of his hard-on was clearly visible in the lightweight fabric. His eyes met hers.

For the first time since Mother died, Tea had the tiny wish to talk to the old lady one more time. A part of her thought she might be connected to Duke now, but if Duke was her Conpar then she would have to figure out what Baron was. Baron was still hers, right? The younger twin *had* to still be hers.

"Duke." Baron's eyes landed on his brother. "I'm going to take a hot bath with Tea. She's covered in flour."

"And apples." She slipped off the counter.

"Why don't you sit on the couch?" Baron took her hand.

"I think I will." Duke scooped up his pants with shaking hands as Tea followed Baron into the bathroom.

Chapter 20

After Baron filled the bathtub in silence, Tea climbed in and sank into the hot water.

"Did you use that ointment I told you to use this morning?" Baron stripped naked. Even though he asked, he seemed lost in thought.

"Yes." She set her head on the back of the ceramic tub. "I'm fine. Don't worry."

"Yeah. Don't worry." Baron didn't speak again. Tea didn't want to break into his deep contemplation. She would let him talk about what just happened when he was ready.

"I don't even know what I'm doing." Baron climbed into the tub and pulled her into his arms. She set her head on his chest above the lapping water. "I've never spent time with a woman that wasn't with Duke. On the Party Base, I was never sober. I don't even remember the women I met. I was a real dick."

"What does that mean?"

"I don't have other words, Tea-cup."

"I mean, we talk together without your brother all the time. We spend time together."

"You're normally wearing clothes," Baron smirked as his gaze dropped to her chest. After a few seconds his smile faded. His soulful blue eyes caught hers. "What did you do different, Tea? How did you get him to come without me? In fact, I didn't even know he was hard. I didn't feel anything. You broke our connection. That's never happened."

"I didn't mean to." Tea's brow wrinkled in confusion. "I didn't mean to change anything." She lifted her head off Baron's chest and stared into the younger twin's eyes. "We were talking in the kitchen, and then we started to fool around. He thought it was your hard-on."

"Trust me when I say that was all him." Baron stared at the door of the bathroom. "And he must've wanted you a lot to dive in like that." Reaching for the bar of soap from the side of the tub, Baron then created bubbles and trailed suds along her back.

"He thought he'd help me get off until you came home. He did sort of dive in without thinking." Tea sat up in Baron's arms as she began washing her body with the cleanser. "We both did."

"That's not like him." Distractedly, Baron spoke but his eyes traveled over her chest a second time. He trailed his fingers through the lather down her neck to her bellybutton.

"I know." Tea grinned. "I've got a pretty good handle on both of you."

"I thought I'd be mad seeing you with him without me." Baron's eyes lifted to her face as he set the bar of soap to the side.

"Are you?"

"No." He moved away from her in the water and stood. "It's crazy but I want him to be happy even if that means I lose you."

Tea expected him to say more, but he didn't. Instead, he stepped out of the tub and grabbed a towel off the rack.

"Do you think you lost me?" Tea rose then stepped out of the tub. Naked and dripping, she moved into his arms stopping him from drying his body.

"I don't know." Baron kissed her cheek. "I wish I knew what this all meant for us. Do you still want me? What am I? Am I the brother of your boyfriend now, or are you still with me?"

"I'm with you." Tea hugged him. "I like you as much as I like Duke." Tea kissed his cheek as she chased away his fears. "I'm with you both."

Tea thought about his concerns as she took the towel from his hands. She was starting to be positive she'd met her match. Both of them.

"Mother was crazy and heartless, but she was smart. She'd been studying matches all her life. She used to say that when you find a soulmate or a Conpar it could affect your gifts. That's how you'd know you met the right person. I didn't change your gift. I may have changed your side effect. Maybe you can have sex apart now."

"Did we change you?"

Tea patted his skin and thought hard about that question. The urge to fight had been with her since the second her gift came into her life. Now she didn't want to do that any longer. She wanted peace. Tea wanted the twins and peace, love, forgiveness.

"You make me feel relaxed. I don't want to fight anymore. I want to be a good person, a better person."

"You were always a good person." Baron kissed her mouth as he took the towel from her arms. He lifted his mouth away as he began to dry her skin.

"I want you." She took the towel from his hands and tossed the terrycloth to the floor. Grabbing his hands, she tugged him toward the bedroom. "We should figure this out. Duke would want us to look at this from all angles." Tea pulled Baron from the bathroom to the bedroom. She stopped at Baron's bed. "We should see if you can come without your brother."

"No." Baron shook his head and untangled his hands from hers. "I think your body might need a break, Tea. I think we're too hard on you. I loved everything we did together last night, but it's okay to hold you and not do anything else. I'm not a monster. I don't want to break you."

"You won't break me, Baron. I'm not fragile." Tea grinned. "I'm not a teacup," she whispered as she sank to the mattress. Tea loved how Baron always worried about her. He may say worry was bad for their health, but that rule never applied to himself.

Sitting on the edge of the bed, Tea's hand zeroed in on his erection. His cock was thick, swollen, and hunting for her. Her fingers slipped up and over the head, then back down.

"Is this yours?"

"Tea," he groaned.

"Can I change your mind? Say the word." She bent her head to lick playfully at his cock.

"Word." Baron moaned when she squeezed him again. "You can do whatever you want."

"You're a pushover." Tea stretched back on the blankets and drew him down next to her.

"Only with you." Baron's eyes followed her hands as she stroked and touched his skin. Once she had him settled on the bed, she pushed his chest until he was flat on his back.

"I know you said you're not much for blowjobs. That's Duke's thing, but I thought I'd taste you." Tea bent over his body and licked again at his cock. The shaft strained toward her. "I thought the two of us could try it out."

"I've never had one." Baron's cheeks flushed.

"Really?"

"It seemed like an off thing to ask someone to do. I had a few offers on the Party Base, but I was out of it. I turned it down. No one wants to suck you off while you're crying into your liquor."

"It's a very Duke action to think about things from all angles and ponder it."

"Ha." Baron chuckled.

Tea licked playfully at his hard-on, and he groaned. He may not ask for it, but she didn't think sucking his dick was something he wouldn't like.

Baron sat up suddenly and grabbed her around her waist. "If this is just the two of us." He flipped her around until she straddled his face. "Then I get to taste you too."

Tea grinned and pressed her chest to the tops of his thighs. Her hands slipped over his legs. The hair on his shins tickled her fingertips.

"I'm on top." She glanced over her shoulder. "You wouldn't want to crush me."

"Ha." Baron got out, but then he moaned when her fingers slid along his balls. "Yes. You're fragile."

Tea's tongue darted out and started at his balls before moving toward his shaft.

Baron's breath hitched when she kissed the head of his cock. The pink tip begged for more as a drop of pre-cum gathered and fell. Tea curled her fingers around the smooth shaft. The weight was like satin, and she liked the shallow way Baron panted as she played with him.

As he pulled her legs apart, Baron's mouth found her clit like he knew where it was without even looking. His tongue bathed the tiny nub of flesh until he had her rocking on his mouth.

Leaning over his shaft, Tea wrapped her mouth around his waiting flesh. Her curiosity awakened. If Baron could come without his brother, she felt like that might mean something important for the three of them. Her hands slid down a little and she squeezed his thigh. Her other hand cupped his balls.

"For the love of…" Baron growled as he pulled his lips from her slit. His voice was a hoarse whisper.

For a moment, Tea sucked, then let the hard shaft slip from her mouth. Next, she licked the base and moved gradually up to the top. Baron's needy cock hardened even more with every touch of her mouth and hands. Running the tip of her tongue around the head, Tea wiggled with surprise when again Baron's mouth clasped tightly on her throbbing lips. He started to suck on her skin before adding a finger to her channel. Tea tried to think about her mouth bobbing on this cock, but his tongue, lips, and fingers made her forget what she was doing. Her nipples rubbed against his leg hair as she swayed against him.

Baron's hips lifted off the bed. He grabbed her ass and squeezed. His other hand continued to use thick fingers to drive her closer and closer to the edge.

Latching onto his dick once more, Tea started to draw the length deep past her tongue. She began a smooth rhythm that had Baron thrusting in time to her suction. His mouth matched hers, suck for suck. His fingers drove her wild. Tea scooted on her knees to get closer to his lips. She wanted more. She needed him. Her hands pulled again at the throbbing flesh. The more she touched Baron, the more he did in return.

The man under her tasted like safety and an essence that was all Baron. There was a power here that she loved.

She drank from it like nectar. The younger twin trembled with need, and she loved that she could make him shudder and moan. Tea continued to suck endlessly. He stroked her, played, and then stroked again. She dipped her head toward the base and then popped back up. Faster and faster, she started to bob her head. Baron's tongue drilled into her, and her fingers began to dance across his balls making him squirm.

"You have to stop." Baron lifted his mouth away from her, but his fingers kept caressing her wet flesh.

Tea paused to let him slip out of her mouth, and she looked over her shoulder. "Why?"

"I think I might…" Baron's brow wrinkled, and his eyes caught hers. "I don't know. This is different."

"Do you really want me to stop or do you want to find out what it's like with just the two of us?"

"Let's find out."

Tea dropped her mouth back on him. In seconds, she had him back to a furious rhythm. Baron returned to her slit. He moaned deeply into her channel as he kept his lips dancing across her clit. The hand on her ass moved to her outer thigh, and he hugged her lower body to him. Baron drank her juices as he relentlessly drew on her needy flesh. Tea matched him. Baron acted like he couldn't stop himself. She didn't want him to. Tea ground down on his face just as her orgasm began.

Grasping at the heat shooting throughout her limbs, her body jolted all the way to her toes.

"Tea." Suddenly, Baron's abs contracted as he shuddered. "I'm going to come." Baron filled her mouth, and his seed headed straight down her throat. He let out a moan as his lips attacked her clit with a vengeance.

Tea's climax was renewed. She kept sucking on Baron as she started to come in surges. Wave after wave hit her.

Her lips stayed on Baron's quivering pulsating flesh. He licked and sucked and drank from her. Tea melted on top of him as pure gratification consumed her.

Right as Tea thought the pleasure would kill her, Baron let go of her clit. She lifted her head and let him slip from her lips. His dick was wet and softening. Tea glanced over her shoulder as her orgasm faded. Sleep took this moment to rear up and demand she comply. A shudder passed down her spine as she dropped her head to his thigh. Baron mumbled out undecipherable words.

"I didn't mean to do that in your mouth. I thought I had more control than that." Baron panted. "It was so fast and strong. It's different without him. I should've done something."

"You did something." Tea smiled and then rose from where she was sprawled over his body. "You did fine."

"How did you do that to me?" Baron looked as confused as Duke did earlier in the kitchen.

Tea couldn't answer how she was doing any of this. All she could think was that after everything that happened, she had finally met her match. Oddly enough, her Conpar happened to be a set of twins.

"I guess you two belong to me." Tea picked up the sheet on the bed and wrapped the cloth around her body. "That means no more prostitutes." She stood and glared at Baron.

"I can't speak for Duke, but, Tea-cup, I'm yours until the day I die." Baron got up from the bed. "I don't want anyone else ever." He wrapped his arms around her waist and set his head onto her shoulder. He hugged her and nuzzled her neck.

"I'm yours too, little Tea," Duke's voice came from behind her. She lifted her head as the older twin leaned in the doorway of the bedroom. "Whether you want us together or separate, we'll do it. We're yours." This time when Baron and Duke shared a silent conversation, she didn't mind.

"If we have to move to get away from the H.S.P.C. so that Tea is never found—" Baron hugged her.

"—then we'll do that," Duke finished.

Chapter 21

Tea set her steaming apple pie on the kitchen counter. The golden-brown crust looked exactly like the pictures in her cookbook. The shade reminded her of the twins' hair color. She grinned at the pastry. After a week of trying, and three disasters, she'd finally made the top and cooked the apples to perfection.

Once she transferred the pie to the cooling rack, she stopped and glanced down at her loose button-down shirt hanging on her frame. Her chest was covered in flour and sugar again. Baron would be home from work in twenty minutes. Tea planned to spend the evening with the boys hopefully eating her pie and then the twins eating her. She wiped off the counter quickly and then headed to the bedroom to change.

On a whim, she showered and then grabbed Duke's huge white fluffy robe from the back of the door. For the past few days, life with her twins was as perfect as her pie. For once, she decided that the world was good. She was good. Everything was good.

Tea hugged the robe to her body as she opened the door to the bedroom.

Snow-Everyone-Joe stood next to the bed.

Their eyes met. Tea gulped down the scream of surprise and panic at seeing the agent in her room. No. This couldn't be the end. Her life couldn't be over already. Her life had just begun.

"Teagan." Joe scratched at a day's growth of beard on his face. He looked exactly like she remembered when he brought her into the H.S.P.C. headquarters. Bright-orange hair, soulless black eyes. An aura of danger hung over him like a second skin.

Tea recoiled from her name. She wasn't Teagan, Mother's right hand. She was Tea, Duke and Baron's match. Her eyes flipped to the door, then back to Joe. The insolent agent's black eyes never left her. He studied her as she did him. They both remembered the fight on the platform when she'd defended Mother. Tea had almost killed Joe, and he'd gotten the better of her. The idea of fighting him made her skin crawl. Something had changed. Because of Duke and Baron, the idea of throwing down, killing, attacking seemed like that was someone else. It wasn't her. Two things had changed her like Mother had said the day she'd met her.

"Are we going to do this?" Joe shifted until he was closer to the door.

Tea shook her head. One of Joe's orange eyebrows lifted.

"Tea. Are you okay?" Baron entered the bedroom and dashed to her side. "For the love of Pete." He wrapped his arms around her and then pushed her behind his back. "You're fast, Joe. I thought you were still at the hospital."

"Well, shit," Joe muttered more to himself as he rocked back on his heels. "You're protecting her. You're not a hostage."

"Zap-my-dangles. I didn't even know you were here."
Duke appeared in the doorway next. "Joe." He crossed the
room and took up a spot next to his brother. "This is
probably—"

"—not what you think or—"

"—if it is, we want to—"

"Wow." Joe cut off the boys' blabbering. "Have her
dress and come to the living room." With that Joe left the
bedroom.

Baron turned around and hugged her. Tears welled in
her eyes, and she buried her head in his chest. Impending
loss stole all the air in her lungs. The twins were her safe
place. They were her peace. To lose them would be the
most painful thing she would ever have to face.

"Here, Tea," Duke's voice rumbled. He held out a gray
sweatshirt and her jeans from the closet. "We won't let
anything happen to you."

"I wish I could stay." She took the clothes as she pulled
out of Baron's warm embrace.

"We'll talk to Joe." Duke took the robe as she pulled
on her clothing. "Joe is a nice guy deep down. Don't let his
scary eyes fool you."

"There is no talking. I can fight or accept. There isn't
anything else." When she was dressed, her eyes met his. "I
get that now."

"Then we'll fight the agents and run." Baron nodded.
"We'll take you anywhere you want, Tea."

"Agents?" she asked.

"Joe came to the apartment with this tall guy with a
ponytail and—" Duke started.

"—with two other men. They were at the hospital
today. A chubby young man and a guy that looks pissed,"
Baron finished.

"We can fight them." Duke agreed with his brother.

For a moment, Tea considered the offer. She'd seen them battle. The twins were no joke, but was she truly considering making the twins go on the run for her? If they attacked agents, their futures would be over. She knew what kind of life they would lead. Train to train, low on food, forever moving. It wasn't a real life.

"No. I've lived like that. I've killed an agent, and I ran. I stayed on the run with Mother. I was hunted. I won't be hunted again. I won't do that to your life. I love you both." Tea had said she loved them during the heat and passion of sex. Now, she knew what that emotion really was. This wasn't lust. These feelings were pure untainted love. She loved the boys more than she loved her freedom. More than she loved herself.

"We will think of a way to keep you." Duke hugged her as they walked toward the door. "I need to look at this from all angles."

"The first time when the H.S.P.C. captured me, I remember walking toward my execution scared. I remember feeling alone. This time," she grabbed Baron's hand, "at least I don't have to die alone."

"You're not going to die." Baron's hands quivered as he reached the bedroom door. "We'll fight before we'll let that happen."

"I'm tired of fighting." Tea shook her head. "I have used my gift to fight and kill, and I never came out on top. I don't want to do that anymore. It doesn't work. This time I'm not going to do any of that. This time I'll go with peace, and maybe by doing that, you both won't get hurt."

"We don't care if—"

"—we get hurt."

"I care. I'll accept going to the H.S.P.C. if you don't get in trouble and they don't hurt you. Peace, love, forgiveness." Maybe that Luna woman wasn't so crazy after all.

"Tea," Baron began. "We need to—"

"—do something."

"If you want to help me, I'd like you to promise me that you'll be there up to my death. I don't want to be alone this time. When I'm with the two of you, I feel safe and at peace. I want that feeling all the way up to the end of my life. Promise me."

Both men nodded, but they didn't look happy. She understood, but she couldn't ruin their lives. She couldn't let them get hurt. Tea wanted to protect them in a way she had never wanted to protect anyone. Not Mother, not her sister, not even herself. Tea would sacrifice everything for them.

"We aren't leaving your side no matter—"

"—what happens next."

Tea opened the bedroom door to the living room and peered out.

Agent Joe leaned against the counter. The same counter she and Duke had had sex on. Next to him was a man, maybe in his late twenties, with short hair and a squished nose. His cheeks flushed red. All eyes looked to her as she entered the room followed by Baron and Duke.

"This is her?" The agent with Joe flashed his glowing gears bracelet marking him as an H.S.P.C. agent. He didn't wait for an answer but spoke in a stern voice. "I'm Agent Oskin. I'm the senior agent in charge of this mission." His eyes glared at Joe and then looked back at her. "I'm here for Teagan."

The door to the apartment opened and in walked the last person Tea expected to see.

"Great. You're back," Oskin said. "This is Arrow. You might know him as 'Weaver.' I'm told that was his title when he was with The Originals."

Tea knew him all too well. Weaver was the harvester Mother had saved and babied. Weaver was part of The Originals just like her. He was supposed to have been killed like her and Mother. Tea wondered how the other Original member had dodged punishment. She had to admit he looked thinner and more emaciated than she recalled. Also, his hair was chopped short. When she knew the tall Native American, he had a long-woven braid that reached his ass. Now his black hair only brushed his shoulders in a ponytail. Apparently, life with the H.S.P.C. had not been kind to him.

"Is Mother alive too?" Panic that the head of The Originals might walk into this room made Tea's voice squeak with alarm.

"No," Joe answered. "I watched the end of that." With those words, Joe moved around the island counter where her pie sat in the middle. He leaned over and inhaled.

"You'll address all your questions to me," Agent Oskin snapped. "I'm the senior agent here. Not Joe."

"We got it the first time." Baron glanced at Joe. Snow-Everyone-Joe didn't even look up from the pie.

"Teagan, you've been sentenced to death for crimes committed with The Originals," Oskin began, as if he'd prepared a memorized speech.

"Who made the apple pie?" Joe cut off the other agent. Oskin's eyes flipped to Joe, and he scowled.

"Don't interrupt me." Oskin's cheeks flushed with anger. "I don't even think you should be here. She's obviously not a threat. I could do this by myself." Oskin paused. "And I have Arthur."

"I'm here to look after Arrow." Joe began to open the cabinets in the kitchen. "I go where Arrow goes." When he found a plate, he looked at the skinny Native American.

Weaver and Tea had been staring at each other up to this point. For Tea, she was reliving the hell of being with Mother and him. She couldn't read what Weaver was thinking. When Joe pointed to the pie, the other man nodded. Joe cut into the pastry.

"As I was saying," Oskin began a second time.

The door to the apartment opened again. A chubby young man in his early twenties with shaggy brown hair entered. His brown eyes nervously scanned the room.

"This is Agent Arthur," Oskin announced with his nose in the air. "He's gifted with the strength to match yours, Teagan. I wanted you to know that in case you get any ideas of escaping your punishment this time."

Arthur stood by the door and scratched at his greasy hair. His eyes landed on Joe and the pie.

"Joe, I thought you said she was dangerous? She can't be more than twenty, and she looks kind of sweet."

"I'm the senior agent here," Oskin snapped. "You will address all questions to me."

"Tea isn't a threat. She is sweet." Duke took a step in front of her. "Please, Joe, listen. You can't take her back to the H.S.P.C. She doesn't even have her gift. She is weak and—"

"—she needs us." Baron pushed her behind his back. "You can't throw her in jail again. They were killing her."

She peered over Baron's shoulder.

"I had read that she lost her gift, but—" Joe started.

"I'm not bringing Teagan into headquarters." Oskin cut Joe off in midsentence and stepped closer to the boys. All eyes turned to the surly agent. "I'm here to execute her as she should have been. I'm in charge. The only reason

Joe's in this room is because Arrow is here to tell me if this is indeed Teagan. The woman with Mother."

"I'm *with* Duke and Baron." Tea found herself whispering. She clutched at Baron's shirt as her eyes prickled with tears. So, she wouldn't even be going back to the hellish white room.

As her eyes misted, they met Joe's. If she had to die somewhere, this was better than any place she could picture. She would be in her home, with her twins. She would do this as long as her twins were safe.

"Is this Teagan?" Oskin demanded of Arrow.

The harvester's eyes flickered over the tears shimmering on her lashes when she stepped between Duke and Baron. He nodded slowly.

"Yea, but Joe…" Arrow's brow puckered.

"If this is her, that's all I need to know," Oskin barked. "I don't want to hear what Snow-Everyone-Joe has to say. His gift of speed isn't needed. You two can leave at any time. Thank you for your assistance, but I can take it from here."

"No," Baron pleaded. "She isn't with The Originals. Our Tea-cup isn't Mother's anything. She is ours."

"Tea-cup?" Joe smirked as he arranged a second slice of pie on his plate.

"Ours?" Arthur asked.

"We want to talk to a council. We want a new hearing," Baron demanded. "A fair one."

"Please." Duke looked from Oskin to Joe. "Consider what you are doing here. Think about this."

"I didn't know Oskin was here to execute her." Joe's eyes met Baron's troubled ones.

Tea placed her hand on Baron's sleeve. She wanted to comfort both the twins, but she was still reeling that this was her end and there wouldn't be a second chance.

"I thought we were here to take her back to H.S.P.C." Arthur ran a huge hand over the pimples on his forehead.

"She's not traveling and having the opportunity to escape again. I'm not authorized to do anything other than finish the sentence that should've been carried out." Oskin spoke like the idea was ridiculous. "She had a hearing. A fair one. I'm not here for negotiations." He took another step forward. "Step aside, Duke and Baron. This is official business. Teagan, step forward."

All eyes turned to Tea.

Chapter 22

Stepping past Baron and Duke, who made a unified front, Tea took a deep, settling breath. It was time she let everything go. If this was her death, she would face her demise with grace. Not anger and not fighting. Fighting never got her anywhere. She would choose peace.

"I've some things I want to say before I go." Tea turned to Joe first. "I'm sorry, Agent Joe, that I tried to kill you." One of his orange eyebrows lifted. "I won't give you my excuse. I simply wanted you to know that Mother wasn't worth protecting."

"Yea," Weaver muttered. "You can say that again."

Tea turned to the harvester next. There was so much history between her and Weaver, and for the first time in her life, she found she could let go that part of her past. She and Weaver were caught in a web of Mother's making. At least he got out and would live and learn. Tea tried not to envy his future.

"I'm sorry for how everything went with us too, Arrow." When she said his name, it brought a smile to his lips. He wasn't "Weaver" any more than she was "Teagan." So much had changed. For a small window of time, Tea had gotten a whole new life. Just as Luna had said. These past weeks had made her whole horrible past worthwhile. Everything she'd been through brought her to these good men.

"Tea." Arrow's head nod said more than any words could.

Finally, Tea studied the man who would execute her. "I need to say goodbye to my twins."

"Fine." Oskin gave an angry, curt head jerk. "If you think the dramatics and the waterworks are going to change anything, then you're wrong. I'm not fooled by your pathetic apologies. Say what you want, but I'm not leaving here until I see this needle enter your body."

Tea turned her back on the agents in the room.

As soon as she did, Duke and Baron enveloped her in a hug. She might suffocate, but she always did think death should be their warm embrace.

"I'm sorry, Duke." Tea's voice was husky with tears. "I'm sorry, Baron." A few drops slipped down her cheeks.

"What do you mean?" Duke asked.

"What do you mean, what do I mean?" As she swiped at the tears on her cheek, she laughed. "I mean I'm sorry. I'm sorry that it has to end between us. I'm sorry I didn't meet both of you sooner. I'm sorry I wasted so much time on a life that wasn't worth living." Tears began to stream down her face. Baron wiped at her cheeks as drops shimmered in his eyes. "I'm sorry for everything. I really did want forgiveness, love, peace. I finally understood it. You taught it to me."

Baron buried his face into her shoulder. "Run, Tea. We'll fight the agents, and you can get out of the base."

"But I can't." She wiped at her eyes and looked from Baron to Duke. "Don't you see? None of it ever worked out that way. Fighting, running, killing. I've done that. None of it ever turned out right. I never became a better person or learned or healed. I never saved anyone, let alone my sister. I didn't even save myself." Tea paused. "Nothing got better until I came here to be with you. You're both so accepting. So patient. I learned that from you." Tea smiled through the wetness on her face. "The first time I met Mother, she said there'd be only two things that would ever bring me peace." She looked at the twins in turn. "It's you. Duke and Baron. I love you, both."

"We can't let this happen," Duke whispered fiercely.

"You have to." Tea took Duke's hand. "I'm thinking this through. I'm looking at it from all angles. If you fight agents, you'll get hurt. If you win, you'll be on the run until you die. You'll be hunted. If you lose, they could kill you. This is how this has to end if I want to keep you safe. Fighting isn't the answer."

"Tea." Duke hugged her.

"Fighting is the answer," Baron mumbled as he did the same. Both men held her as if they would never let her go. She held on to that feeling.

"I'm ready." Tea pulled out of the twins' arms and looked to Oskin.

"Finally," Oskin grumbled.

"I don't get this," Agent Arthur spoke from in front of the exit he appeared to be guarding. "I thought you said she was a hardened criminal. I thought you said she'd attack me. She's basically some fragile woman. She's crying."

"Oh, she's not fragile," Joe scoffed at his plate.

"She's with The Originals." Oskin frowned at the other agent.

"For the last time, she's not with The Originals. She's—" Duke began as he moved to stand between her and Oskin.

"—*with* us," Baron finished as he took up a spot next to his brother. "No one else. We won't let you touch her."

"Wow." Joe pulled two forks out of one of drawers. He handed one to Arrow.

"Now that's true." Arrow slid the pie plate closer before he sat on the stool.

"You can go." Oskin glared at Joe cutting another slice of pie.

"I'm eating." Joe took a huge bite and grinned at the agent.

Oskin huffed and then turned to Duke and Baron. "Stand aside. If you make one move to stop me, Agent Arthur and I will take you into H.S.P.C. headquarters for obstructing an agent in the course of his duty." Oskin looked to Arthur near the door. "You can arrest Duke and Baron. They should be brought in since they hid a dangerous criminal. We can bring them in after Teagan is dead."

The twins didn't move, but neither did Arthur. The young agent glanced to Joe, then Arrow, and then his eyes landed on her. He appeared to be sweating. The young agent's skin looked glossy with an oily sheen. Stains of water appeared under his arms. He mopped his brow.

"Joe?" Arthur asked.

"I'm the senior agent here." Oskin's voice rose an octave.

Tea cleaned the tears on her face with her sleeve. She noticed out of the corner of her eye that Joe rolled his eyes.

"I'll go along with whatever happens, but I want a promise that nothing bad will happen to the twins." Tea addressed Oskin first. "I don't want the twins in trouble because I stayed here." She turned to face Joe. "I'd like your word. I won't fight, but I want them safe."

"Why his word?" Oskin asked.

Joe took another bite of the apple pie. He stared up at the ceiling. "Why me?"

"Because the twins trust you. So, I do."

"Wow." Joe shrugged. "Alright, Tea. You got it. You have my word that the twins won't be in trouble. They'll stay here in their home. Consider it house arrest."

"You can't promise that," Oskin sputtered.

"Don't push me, Oskin." Joe's black eyes glittered.

"It doesn't matter. Teagan will be dead, and that's the mission I was sent here to do." Oskin produced a needle from his coat. He set the syringe on the counter. At the sight of the instrument what would end her life, she stepped backward. Immediately, Duke wrapped an arm around her. Baron stood in front of her.

"I don't get it. Teagan is your girlfriend?" Arthur scanned them from the doorway. The chubby young man looked back and forth. "She's your girlfriend. Which one?"

"Both of us." Duke nodded.

"Both?" the young agent asked.

"Yes." Baron looked at Duke. They were sharing one of their silent conversations and appeared to be barely paying attention.

"But there are two of them. Isn't that gross?"

"I don't need the commentary." Oskin frowned at the agent. "I only have you here to protect me from a violent and strong gifted Original member."

"Even if she's pregnant and her heartstrings are tied to these men?" Arrow asked.

Chapter 23

For the second time, everyone looked at Tea. She didn't have an answer to whether she was pregnant or not. She'd had sex with both the twins. She could be carrying their child. Fresh tears spurted. She would never meet their children. Tea took a deep breath to keep her calm. Again, she wiped her face with her sleeve.

"Are you pregnant?" Arthur's eyes dropped to her belly, and then he turned to Joe. "Is she tied to them?"

"It doesn't matter. I won't listen to more heartstring explanations," Oskin announced.

"Wow, if you think heartstrings don't matter, you have a lot to learn, Senior Agent," Joe muttered to his pie.

"But we are tied together?" Tea's eyes jumped to Arrow. He knew as much about Mother's beliefs in a Conpar as she did. Tea had the feeling he knew even more.

"Your heartstrings are evenly divided between both the twins. You're their perfect match." Arrow's eyes danced over her like he saw more than her body. His ponytail fluttered. "They're tied to you and you to them." Arrow's eyes flipped to Joe.

"It doesn't matter," Oskin repeated. "We are to follow the H.S.P.C. dictate." Oskin held up the needle and waved it around. "This syringe will give you a painless and quick death. It will be swift judgment." Agent Oskin pulled out a sheet of paper from his coat. "I will now read your sentencing."

"It matters to me," Arthur snapped as he ran his hands through his greasy hair. "Joe, this doesn't seem right. We have women dying of Snow Flu everywhere, and we're planning to kill a healthy female who can give birth? What if we kill her and she is carrying a baby now? I won't be a party to that."

"Joe is not in charge of the mission." Oskin slapped the needle down on the counter. He then cleared his throat and looked at the paper in his hand. "I will now read the sentencing."

"I'll give Tea the injection. She's afraid of needles," Baron said suddenly. He stepped forward and grabbed the syringe off the counter. "I don't want you touching her. No one is touching her but me."

"Here we go." Joe leaned against the counter.

"Hand that back right now, or you'll be arrested for interrupting official H.S.P.C. business," Oskin bit out.

"I'll get it." Duke reached for the needle and shoved Baron. Baron stumbled backward. "You're too hasty. You could hurt her. Give it back to the agent." Grabbing the front of Baron's shirt, Duke pulled back his arm for a punch.

"He *might* hurt her. I *know* you would."

"I would not," Duke growled. "If anyone should hold Tea while she dies, it's me." Duke grappled to snatch the drug out of Baron's hand. "Give me the needle."

"I signed for her." Baron caught his brother's fist and flung his hand back. The younger twin struck Duke in the stomach. Duke doubled over.

Tea shifted closer to the counter as her forehead wrinkled in confusion. She'd not seen the boys brawl since they started to have sex. After she was gone, is this what their lives would return to?

Baron elbowed Duke in the face. Blood poured out of the older twin's nose. She shook her head sadly. The twins' lives would go back this after she was dead.

"I let the messenger go so we could keep her." Duke dove at Baron and tackled him to the floor.

Tea got ready to call out to them. They were upset, but this was no way to handle the deep river of emotions. If only there was some way to give them a little peace before she left.

"Timeout." Tea held up her hand. For the first time, the twins didn't acknowledge her. She whistled. Everyone looked at her but the twins. Baron nailed Duke in the ribs. Duke backhanded him. Blood dribbled from Baron's mouth. He spat the red glob to the floor.

After weeks of learning when a fight would escalate, Tea edged closer to the counter between the stools. She climbed up on the seat, shoved the pie closer to Joe, and then crawled to the middle of the marble. Joe eyed her as she sat cross-legged on the center of the island.

"What are you doing?" Arrow asked.

Right as the words left Arrow's mouth, Baron tackled his brother. Duke hit the stool that the other man was perched on. The chair leg splintered from impact. Arrow flipped to the floor. Glue pieces littered the cement. Arrow sprawled next to the counter.

Joe offered Arrow his hand. "I think I know why Teagan sits up there."

"I don't want to get knocked over."

"Move over here." Joe pulled Arrow to the other side of the counter as Duke grabbed Baron around the waist. The older twin went for the back of Baron's leg. The hard yank pulled one of Baron's legs out from under him.

When Baron was on his back, he kicked wide. Duke sidestepped. The strike caught Oskin's knee. The agent howled in pain and then jumped out of the way of the fight. Arthur pushed Oskin behind him against the door.

"Get in there and get my injection back," Oskin snapped at Joe. The boys hit the table and the battery went flying. Tea gasped. They struck the table leg so hard the support gave. Duke kicked Baron as the battery crashed to the floor. "Use your gift of speed," Oskin said from behind Agent Arthur's back.

"I'm not the senior agent." Joe climbed up on one of the counters and picked up his pie plate. He took another huge bite.

Duke and Baron didn't seem to hear the conversation. Baron tackled Duke again and flipped him over the couch. Strangling each other, they crashed into the coat rack next to the bedroom door. Coats and sweaters scattered in all directions.

Oskin looked at Arrow.

"I'm only here to tell you that this is Teagan." Arrow did the same thing as Joe. He got up on the counter as the boys rolled by pounding each other in the face.

"Agent Arthur." Oskin looked reluctant to lose his shield. "Do something about this."

"I'm not stepping between those two." Arthur winced when Baron put Duke in a headlock. Duke gasped for air as he brought his arm up in a sharp uppercut. They spun until Duke was on top. "I'm not even sure I can do this. I don't want to kill a fragile woman."

"She isn't fragile." Oskin yelled. "Teagan is a highly dangerous criminal who dodged punishment, and we are to carry out the sentence before she gets away again. She could escape and kill people." Oskin stepped to the side of Arthur when the twins hit the bookcase. The shelves gave. The floor filled with books and gadgets. The sound was deafening. Tea cringed at the damage.

Tea took a deep breath. She didn't want this to be her last moments with the twins. The last thing she would remember should not be a brawl.

"Timeout." She sighed. The twins froze. Duke's arms still strangled Baron's neck. "I don't want this to be our last moment together."

"We don't want this to be our last moment with you at all." Duke shoved Baron away from him. "We thought if we gave you the injection, then perhaps it could all be okay."

Baron lifted himself off the floor. Blood streaked his mouth and chin. "We don't want anyone to hurt you. If we must accept this, then we have to make sure that we're taking care of you—"

"—all the way until the end."

The two of them limped to the counter. Baron helped her off the marble, and Duke hugged her as he wiped the blood from his face.

"Give me a proper goodbye and do the injection quick."

"I should do it," Oskin snapped.

"You really want to fight with the twins about it?" Joe asked.

"Give me another piece of pie." Arrow gestured to the pastry.

As Joe began cutting, Baron and Duke turned to her. They glared only once at Oskin to back off, and then Duke kissed her lips softly.

"I have to tell you that I love you. No perhaps, no probably. There are no angles. I love you." Duke hugged her tightly to her chest. "The day you showed up in that box was the best day of my life. I should've said it before. I didn't know how. I'm not so good at talking to women." He grinned but no happiness reached his eyes.

Tea smiled. "You do fine."

"I love you too." Baron pulled her into his embrace next. He kissed her lips softly, then wiped a fresh tear from her cheek. "I will love you until I die. I thought you would ask me to fight for you. I realize that not fighting for you is much harder." His lips pressed into a hard line, and his Adam's apple bobbed. "I would do anything for you. Say the word."

"Word." A sob broke from her at the sweet words from both men. "I love you, both. I'll miss you."

"We will—"

"—see you again."

Tea nodded and closed her eyes.

"What the hell is going on?" Arthur threw up his meaty hands as more sweat covered his face. The wetness now soaked his shirt from the neck down. "You're just going to eat pie while they kill their maybe-pregnant girlfriend?" The agent stared incredulously at Joe and Arrow. "Doesn't anyone see how insane this is? What happened to the heartstring stuff?" he asked Arrow.

Arrow didn't answer but looked to Joe.

Arthur glanced at Joe as well. "What happened to the speeches the H.S.P.C. gave about protecting life?" The fuming agent turned to Oskin last. "The name stands for

Human Survival and Population Care. I never signed up for murder."

"There are some criminals that cannot be ignored. We follow orders," Oskin intoned.

"Well, shit, if you're Oskin, then you follow orders blindly." Joe gave a pointed look at the agent.

"I can't be a part of this hypocrisy. I'm not killing a pregnant woman." With that announcement, Arthur spun on his heel and headed out the door of the apartment.

"Get back here, Agent Arthur," Oskin yelled, but the man was long gone. Oskin flipped around again and looked at the twins. "Fine. Give Teagan the injection. I'm done with you two." He was clearly not happy about the situation, but Tea didn't care. She simply prepared herself for the end of her life. She had the twins at her side. That was enough.

"Tea, are you ready?" Duke asked.

"I know I am," Joe drawled. "Let's get a move on."

Baron glared at Joe before he turned to face Tea. She was still in Duke's arms.

"Think about how much we love you. Keep your mind on that. We'll always protect you. Close your eyes. Duke will hold you." Baron shifted to her side.

Tea blinked back the tears. She took one last longing look at both the twins and then closed her eyes. She held on to the feel of Duke's arms around her. Baron linked his fingers with hers. The bite of pain on the back of her arm surprised her, but she held on to the feel of the twins holding her close. Duke kissed her as dizziness stole her breath. She waited for her heart to stop beating.

Chapter 24

Tea thought death would be more... comfortable.

Slowly consciousness nudged her and told her in no uncertain terms that she was alive. *Take that, God.* She'd made it again. Tea worked to move or roll over as the ache near her ass started to throb in earnest. Nothing happened. Panic robbed her of her joy. The world came into focus, but all she saw was a sheet of white. Her back continued to throb. Was she in Hell? Heaven? Where was she?

Duke's voice penetrated her confusion. "We're not letting you—"

"—take Tea's body," Baron finished.

Her body? They thought she was dead? Tea's panic intensified. She fought to scream out that she was still alive. She strained to move, to run. Nothing happened.

"Wow," that was Joe's cynical drawl, "are you now?"

"I'll look after the cremation process." That was Baron's voice. "We have an End-Of-Life Center at the hospital." Tea guessed the younger twin was close to where she was prone on the couch. She guessed the white over her eyes was a bedsheet. Her heart thundered in her chest. "I'll make sure you get the ashes after she's incinerated."

Tea tried a second time to scream. Incinerated alive would be horrific. If she could've moved, she would have shaken with fear. That would be a horrendous death. *Please, please*, she begged. No sound came out.

"I'm not leaving. I'm the senior agent here." She knew that was Oskin.

Whatever white fabric that was over her face, suddenly it was gone. Tea found herself looking at the ceiling of the twins' apartment. She had no idea what happened other than she remembered the needle. All she knew was that she couldn't turn her head.

Duke and Baron came and went from her line of sight. They stood making a unified front. They shared another silent conversation. Tea wanted to tell them she was alive and beg them not to let Joe have her incinerated.

"I know you're the senior agent," Baron snapped. "And we don't care what your title is. We're keeping Tea's body."

"She's *with* us." Duke glanced over his shoulder at her. "You can fight us for her."

"Oskin," Joe's voice rumbled. "Without Arthur, you might find fighting the twins not so easy. I'd suggest you go and talk to your partner. You stayed until you saw the needle enter Teagan. Arrow, why don't you go with Oskin? You need a break. I'll meet you back at headquarters after I have Teagan's ashes."

There was a brief silence. Tea couldn't see anything but Baron's and Duke's backs. Dishes abruptly clattered in the sink. The stool scratched against the floor. Once more, she tried to scream or plead for her life. Nothing happened. Not even one muscle moved.

"Fine," Oskin snapped. There were footsteps, then the sound of a door opening and closing.

"I'll see you back at HQ, Joe." That was Arrow's voice. The door made a click.

Tea worked to blink, so they would know she was alive.

The hush over the room resumed. A stool scratched against the floor again. She could hear the twins breathing.

"You're not taking the body," Baron growled. "You can leave."

"We mean it, Joe," Duke added. They didn't walk away from her. The back of Duke's knee touched her arm when he shifted closer to the couch. "We'll send you the ashes."

Joe laughed. The snicker was a light sound, and she didn't know what that meant.

"You're not going to incinerate her. She isn't dead." Joe appeared in her line of sight. He shoved more pie into his face. "How long will she be like this?" Joe snapped his fingers before her nose. The agent's eyes flipped from Baron to Duke. They all leaned over her face.

"Maybe five to ten minutes." Baron scooped her up in his arms. Tea felt relief flood her body. *Thank God.* They all knew she wasn't dead. She wouldn't be incinerated. Except Joe knew. Damn.

"How did you know she was alive?" Duke and Baron settled her between them on the couch. She still couldn't move, but she could see Joe in front of the sofa.

"My eyes can move as fast as the rest of me, but you did a pretty good job. Oskin thinks she's dead."

"You saw what we did?" Baron asked.

"I saw you switch the needles when you knocked over the coat rack. What did you give her?"

Tea was arranged in Duke's lap as Baron got up from the couch. From this angle, she could see more of the apartment. Baron walked over to the scattered coats. He pulled a needle out of the pocket of his work coat. Shaking his head, he handed the syringe to Joe.

"I gave Tea the best immobilization drug the hospital has." Baron inclined his head toward Joe's hand. "That's the injection Oskin had." He looked at her. She wished she could tell him thank you.

"Why didn't you say anything?" Duke asked Joe.

"Because this was wrong from the beginning. I've never seen such a clusterfuck at HQ." Joe crossed his arms over his muscled chest. "First, she isn't given a fair trial. I was busy with Arrow, but I saw that the council was busier with their prestige than their fairness." Joe's eyes stared at hers. "Second, she goes missing and someone at HQ finds out that she's been used as a live test subject. Those doctors were in some real shit when that came to light. Gears had a fit. What they did was against everything the H.S.P.C. stands for."

"She was tortured." Baron moved in front of her.

"Damn straight, she was," Joe growled. "It was wrong, and I think it came down to the fact that no one wanted to face that they'd fucked up. So, her sentence was death. HQ wanted to dust this under the rug, but that's not how I run."

"But you said you didn't know that they were going to kill her."

"I didn't know until Oskin said it. I hoped to get her a new hearing. A fair one just like you said." Joe moved to her side and squatted. He waved his hand over her face, and she blinked. "Arrow wanted you to have a fair hearing. He complained about it to everyone. He likes to bitch."

"Are you going to give her a new trial?" Baron asked.

"No." Joe stood.

"I won't let you give her that injection." Duke cradled her to his chest. If she could have done anything, she would have snuggled into his arms. At this point, all she concentrated on was blinking.

She fluttered her eyelids and wanted to cheer.

"I know you won't." Joe set his dish on the counter. "You can't harm your match. Arrow said it's literally impossible to hurt a Conpar. That's how he knew you wouldn't hurt her. I knew something was up the moment you said you'd give her the injection." Joe began to restlessly pace in front of her. He looked at his watch. Tea winked one eye, and then her hand shifted. She worked to lift both her arms.

"Tea-cup." Baron came to her side and held her hand. She squeezed, and he squeezed her fingers back.

"Are we going to have to fight you, Joe?" Baron turned around to face the agent. Joe's speed and abilities were well known. Her heart started to pound. "We will."

"Not unless you do this my way."

"What way is that?" Duke asked.

"I meant it when I said you're on house arrest. You two are stuck here. I don't want to hear about you leaving. If either of you breathes near a train, I'll be all over you like ice on the Earth."

"Stuck here with Tea?" Baron spoke slowly.

"Wow, catching on," Joe smirked. "You have to stay on the edge of the base. No one hangs this way, so you can hide her better. You keep going to the hospital. You get the batteries done. Keep your heads down."

"What about Oskin?" Duke asked.

"The senior agent," Baron grumbled.

"I'll get some human ashes to turn in to him." Joe paced, and Tea began to move her head to watch the way Joe restlessly strolled back and forth. His eyes met hers. "She isn't leaving this base. I want to know where Tea is at all times. I'll keep an eye on all three of you. Consider yourselves all arrested, and this," Joe made a circle with his finger, "is your new prison."

Tea nodded.

"And," Joe continued, "I better not hear of any Original members around her. No more visits from Silo. She better be a fucking saint."

"I will be." Tea finally got the words out. "Thank you."

"I don't need thanks," Joe scoffed.

Duke and Baron looked at her and smiled.

Joe came over and stared down at her where she sat in Duke's lap. She tipped her head up.

"How long since you've been able to kill the twins and run away?" Joe asked.

"Tea isn't gifted," Baron answered.

"She's fragile," Duke sputtered out. "She could barely walk when she got here."

Tea pulled out of Duke's arms and rose from the couch. She walked around to the back of the sofa next to the fallen battery. Stretching her stiff arms, she paced by the door. Finally, she took a deep breath and looked at the agent.

"Since right after I had sex with the twins the first time." She paused. "I would never kill them though."

"You can't." Joe grinned.

Duke and Baron stared at her. Even with that immobilization drug lingering in her system, she bent over and picked up the huge metal battery. She easily carried the giant tube over to the marble counter and set it on top. Her eyes met Joe.

"How did you know that I had my gift?" she asked.

"You dug your fingers into the marble counter." Joe pointed to the indentations.

"Tea is stronger than us?" Baron sputtered.

"She could crush you like a bug." Joe headed to the door. "But I'm counting on you two to keep her in line. You have my rules. No Original members and you aren't leaving here. You also need a new name. Teagan is dead. Oskin saw it."

"And he's Senior—" Baron began.

"—Agent on this mission," Duke finished.

Joe chuckled.

"I'd like to be Teresa," Tea said. "Tea for short."

"Teresa Farone." Joe shrugged. "Fine with me."

"Why Farone?" Tea looked from Joe to Baron and Duke.

"Because that's the twins' last name," Joe smirked. "Maybe you should know someone's name before you have sex with them." He reached for the door handle. "Anyway, Tea, I'll be back in one year to check on you. I'll expect another pie."

Tea glanced around the kitchen. The pie was gone. She didn't care. She would be alive and able to make a hundred pies with the twins.

"One year," she repeated.

"In the meantime, I'll be watching this base. If anything looks wrong or I hear about anything, I'll be here to kill you before you even know it." The words were a dark promise. Gift or no gift, she knew Joe would do what he vowed.

Tea scanned her twins. Joe's declaration wasn't scary. She had a new life, a new name, and she would be a saint. This was a game she wanted to play. If staying here and being good is what it took, then she would do it. Her family was worth protecting. Her men were worth everything.

Tea turned back to tell Joe that she would pledge to be a decent, moral person, but he was gone. The door to the apartment was closed. She hadn't even heard it open.

Turing around, Tea looked at Duke and Baron. They held their arms out for her.

Duke came to her side and wrapped an arm around her shoulder. "So, you could probably pick up all my batteries?"

"Not probably. I could." Tea laughed. "You said I couldn't help in the storeroom because everything would be too heavy."

Duke laughed.

"Nothing wrong with your memory." Baron wrapped an arm around her waist and kissed her.

"I have to get scarves to cover up the scar around your neck." Baron looked thoughtful.

Duke smiled. "You can tell Mather I want to be a cross-dresser this time."

Tea hugged the boys to her. Duke groaned when she squeezed him extra tight. She was so happy. The joy spilled out of her.

"I love you both."

"We love—" Baron started.

"—you, Tea," Duke finished.

Epilogue

One year later…

The knock on the door gave Tea time to arrange the blanket over her body. She pulled the fabric up to her chin. Sitting on the couch, she looked at Duke. He slowly headed toward the entrance of the apartment. When he reached the door, his eyes flipped back at her.

Tea nodded and then took a deep breath to prepare for Snow-Everyone-Joe. She was ready. The agent said he would be back on this day. His apple pie was cooling on the counter.

Duke opened the door with a swing of his arms. "Joe."

Joe marched in and headed directly to the counter. He didn't look at her even though he said he was going to check on her specifically. Instead, he cut a huge piece of pie, placed the pastry on a plate, and then grabbed a fork. Once he had the dish in hand, he headed over to where she lounged on the couch. His eyes scanned her, then flipped around the room.

"You cleaned."

"It needed a woman's touch." Tea nodded, but actually, she couldn't take all the credit. The twins had stopped fighting. Their last brawl was the day Teagan died. Now, all that was left was Teresa, also known as Tea. She and the boys had spent a lot of time turning their apartment into a home. No longer were the rooms filled with broken furniture.

Joe walked around the couch eating. He stopped at the dining-room table. The chairs were neatly pushed in, and a vase of flowers sat in the center of the wood.

"Moved the batteries to the workroom?"

"Tea liked them there. She wanted to eat at the dinner table, and since she can lift them…" Duke grinned at her. "It's not easy to fight with her about it."

Tea smiled back.

Joe nodded. "Where's the baby?"

Duke jumped, and her shoulders dropped. She'd hoped Joe wouldn't figure that out, but it was a wish in vain. He was after all a famous agent for a reason.

"Baron," Tea called.

"Is he gone?" Baron's head ducked out the bedroom and then his eyes alighted on Joe. "For the love of Pete."

"Where's the baby?" Joe asked Baron.

Moments later, Baron came out of the other room with their little boy. He handed the child to Joe.

As soon as Joe had the kid in his hands, their second child cried from the bedroom. Duke groaned.

"Tess is up." Duke left her with Baron and Joe.

Joe bounced the boy and snuggled him into his arms. Baron watched him intently.

"I'm not going to hurt him. I like babies. They're better than adults." Joe cooed to the child then handed him to Tea. Her little one squirmed in her arms. She rocked him before she began to breastfeed. Joe picked up his pie and sat at the counter.

"So, what's his name?" Joe laughed to himself. "Let me guess, king or emperor? I'm sure he has to be named like Duke and Baron, right?"

"I named him." Duke came out of the bedroom and handed their daughter to Baron. "His name is Volt. It's got a powerful ring to it."

"But now I think Emperor would've been better." Baron rocked their baby girl in his arms. "I bet you didn't even consider that."

"And her?" Joe pointed to their girl.

"Countess." Tea smiled.

"I named her." Baron grinned with pride. "We call her Tess."

"Congratulation on twins. Life is funny like that." Joe finished his pie and then stood from the stool. "Twins are a handful. I guess God has a sense of humor. Maybe they'll fight as much as you two do."

"We never—" Duke began.

"—fight," Baron finished.

"Wow, someone finally relaxed you two." Joe started for the door, and then he stopped. "I've heard nothing about this base. Well done, Tea. I'll be back next year. Nice scarf."

"I'll make more pie." Tea smoothed the knot on the thick blue scarf covering her scar.

"Oh and…" Joe opened the door. "I brought you something." The agent pointed out into the hall with his thumb. "It's bedframes."

~ The End ~

About the Author

C.M. Moore is a retired soldier, and a romantic at heart. After being blown up in Afghanistan and receiving a purple heart, he began writing with his wife. Connor's first book *1:05 am* is a mixture of love, sex, and action.

Today if you are looking for Connor, you can find him volunteering with veteran organizations, and harassing his military buddies.

You can also find him attempting to "hunt" in the woods and ponds of Minnesota. In the event you find him in the woods, don't be scared, he can't hit anything.

If you want to contact him message him at c.m.moore.author@gmail.com

Find out when the next book comes out!
Connect with C.M.Moore:

Facebook:
https://www.facebook.com/profile.php?id=10001044
2116825

Goodreads:
https://www.goodreads.com/author/show/7397933.
C_M_Moore

Pinterest:
https://www.pinterest.com/cmmooreauthor/

Website:
http://www.authorcmmoore.com/

There will be at least 12 novels in the ICE ERA
CHRONICLES and 10 novellas in the OFF-THE-RAILS
ICE ERA CHRONICLES. Want more time in the snow?
Get a FREE Novella! Join the exclusive readers group for
GIVEAWAYS, Advanced reader opportunities and Pre-
order notifications!
Join us:
http://eepurl.com/dnoLrr

Other Books by C.M.Moore

Ice Era Chronicles (In Chronological Order)

1:05 a.m. (Ice Era Chronicles) Book 1

Grinding My Gears (An Off-the-Rails) Ice Era Chronicles Book 1:30 a.m.

2:05 a.m. (Ice Era Chronicles) Book 2

Raiden Out The Storm (An Off-the-Rails) Ice Era Chronicles Book 2:15 a.m.